SOME BUNNY
❤ ❤ TO LOVE ❤ ❤

SOME BUNNY
TO LOVE

MICHELLE SCHUSTERMAN

Scholastic Inc.

FOR TEDDY, LUCY, AND ADI

Copyright © 2021 by Michelle Schusterman
Photos © Shutterstock.com

ISBN 978-1-338-67237-4

10 9 8 7 6 5 4 3 2 1   21 22 23 24 25

Printed in the U.S.A. 40
First printing 2021

Book design by Keirsten Geise
Map illustration © 2021 by Jennifer Kalis

 **LAURA**

The bells hanging over the entrance to JAL Corner Deli jangled. Laura Rodriguez held her breath as footsteps made their way down the center aisle.

She was sitting cross-legged on the floor, completely surrounded by the display tower she'd built from cases of Black Cherry Fizz, a new brand of soda her parents had picked up from the wholesalers. All Laura could see aside from the red and black cases was a strip of fluorescent light overhead.

Quietly, she turned her phone over in her lap so the screen was facedown. The footsteps passed right by the tower, and Laura smiled as they headed toward the dairy section in the back.

Then they stopped, and she suppressed a groan.

Clomp. Clomp. Clomp.

A moment later, her father's twinkling brown eyes peered down at her from the opening at the top of the tower.

"Gotcha!"

"Aw," Laura grumbled, carefully getting to her feet without bumping into the cases. "It took me almost an hour to build this thing, and you found me in less than a minute?"

"Well, I knew you wouldn't try hiding in the ice cream freezer again," Dad joked, and Laura rolled her eyes. Her parents loved to bring up the freezer story, even though it was six years ago. She'd lasted all of ten seconds huddled next to a few pints of mint chocolate chip before frantically scrambling out, and the bodega's security camera had caught the whole thing.

Dad helped Laura shift a stack of cases just

enough so that she could squeeze out of the tower. They'd just finished sliding the stack back into place when the bells jangled again.

"Morning, Jorge!" came a familiar, booming voice. Laura straightened up, brushing her hands off on her denim shorts as Dad stepped forward.

"Ah, Mr. Patel!" he said, heading for the register. "Glad you stopped by—we just stocked more of that ginseng drink you were asking about last week. I set aside a few bottles for you."

"Wonderful, thank you!" Mr. Patel tapped his bearded chin as he wandered down the canned goods aisle. "Now, what was it I came in for?"

A bottle of peach tea, a pack of spearmint gum, and today's paper, Laura thought, but she kept quiet and tidied up the magazine display. Mr. Patel owned Roti Palace across the street, and he always pretended to forget what he was looking for when he stopped by before opening up the restaurant. Besides, if Laura spoke up, then Mr. Patel would start asking her lots of questions, probably about what books she'd read this week. And then Laura would stammer and stumble her way through answering, like her mouth had forgotten how to put together sentences, which was what always happened when she talked to anyone other than her parents and her best friend, Melissa.

The bells jangled again, and Laura heard the husky laugh that belonged to Mrs. Ruiz, the owner of Cada Palabra, East Harlem's newest bookstore. It had just opened earlier that summer, right when school had let out, and in the last two months, Laura spent almost more time there than she had in her family's bodega. Cada Palabra had three whole shelves dedicated to fantasy novels, many of which were by authors from Central and South America. Thanks to Mrs. Ruiz, Laura's list of favorite fantasy authors had doubled.

Laura was trying to gather up the courage to ask Mrs. Ruiz if the latest book in the Encanto Chronicles series had arrived yet when the bodega door swung open again. Three teenage girls walked in, all talking at once, and Laura hurried to the back of the store and busied herself rearranging bags of chips.

"Do you sell phone chargers?" one of the girls asked Laura's dad.

"Right here," Dad replied cheerfully, and Laura pictured him gesturing at the rack to the left of the register. As he rang up the girl's purchase, he called out, "Looking for something in particular, Mrs. Ruiz?"

"Actually, yes!" The bookstore owner sounded slightly out of breath. "I'm in the middle of baking a cake for my niece's birthday party this afternoon, and I realized I forgot to buy sugar, of all things."

"Aisle three, left shelf, bottom row," Dad replied immediately.

Laura froze, the bag of salt and vinegar chips crinkling in her grip. Mrs. Ruiz had been to the bodega only a few times. Did she know about—

"*Eeek!*"

At the sound of her shriek, Mr. Patel's head

whipped around, the group of girls gasped, and Dad raced out from behind the register. But Laura reached aisle three first.

"It's okay!" Laura cried, hurrying toward Mrs. Ruiz, who had just dropped a bag of sugar. "That's just Evie!"

Laura knelt down right in front of the empty space where the bag of sugar had been. Cowering at the back of the shelf was a fuzzy gray bunny, trembling from the tips of her ears to her fluffy tail.

"Oh my goodness," Mrs. Ruiz said, sounding relieved. "I'm so sorry for screaming like that."

Dad joined them and picked up the bag of sugar. "No apologies necessary, Mrs. Ruiz! My fault—Evie's favorite hiding spot is behind the sugar. I should have warned you."

"This is your first time meeting the JAL Corner Deli mascot, I take it?" Mr. Patel called, his eyes twinkling with laughter.

"Indeed it is." Mrs. Ruiz watched as Laura gently scooped Evie up and cuddled her. The bunny's heart was racing a mile a minute, and Laura gently stroked her head. Her stomach dropped when the teen girls all rushed over, cooing and snapping pictures with their phones.

"She's just adorable!" Mrs. Ruiz said. "I've met more than a few bodega cats, but I can't say I've ever met a bodega bunny."

"Laura here loves cats, but she's very allergic," Dad explained, placing a hand on Laura's shoulder. She was hotly aware that all eyes were on her, and her heart had started racing almost as fast as Evie's. "For years, she begged us for a cat, anyway. She said it would be worth all the sneezing!"

"Dad . . ." Laura whispered, her face burning as the girls giggled.

"My wife, Adriana, volunteers at the animal shelter over on 110th Street," Dad continued. "One day a woman came in with a litter of bunnies that needed homes, and we thought it was the perfect solution."

"That's just wonderful." Mrs. Ruiz smiled down at Laura, who managed a weak smile back. All she wanted was to run upstairs to her room with Evie and escape all these staring eyes.

"You can follow Evie on Twitter!" Mr. Patel said jovially. "It's @JALBodegaBunny. Right, Laura?"

The girls were giggling again. Laura wanted to sink through the floor.

"Right," she whispered. Evie had thirty-one followers on Twitter, including @RotiPalaceHarlem.

"I had a bunny when I was little!" one of the girls exclaimed. "She used to do binkies all the time."

"Binkies?" her friend repeated.

"Yeah! It's this jumpy, twirly thing bunnies do when they're happy." The girl looked eagerly at Laura. "Evie probably does them, too, doesn't she?"

Laura nodded wordlessly.

After a moment of awkward silence, Dad spoke up. "She usually does them if you offer her a raspberry. That's her favorite food."

"Oooh, can we try it?"

Clutching Evie, Laura watched as the girl hurried over to the produce and grabbed a box of raspberries. *It's not going to work*, Laura wanted to say. *Please just leave and stop staring at us.*

Instead, she set poor Evie on the floor, and everyone circled around her. The girl held up a raspberry so that Evie could see.

"Do a binky! Come on, you can do it!"

But Evie just trembled. Laura knew exactly how she felt. Bunnies only did binkies when they were totally overjoyed. And how could anyone feel that kind of joy when everyone was staring at them? This girl could hold a handful of jalapeño popcorn under Laura's nose right now, but she definitely wouldn't jump for joy.

"I think she's feeling a bit shy," Dad said at last, and the girl sighed, handing him the raspberries.

"It's okay," she said, patting Evie's head. "Maybe next time!"

Laura picked Evie up, breathing a sigh of relief as everyone returned to what they'd been doing. Dad returned to the register, and Laura hung back as the girls and Mr. Patel paid for their items. Dad's phone buzzed as Mrs. Ruiz approached the register, and Laura could hear him talking to someone in a low voice as the bookstore owner paid for her sugar.

Don't ask about book club, Laura thought silently, crossing her fingers. *Please don't ask about book club . . .*

Mrs. Ruiz was halfway out the door, then suddenly turned around. "Oh, will I see you Saturday, Laura? Our fantasy book club is up to seven members! I really think you'd enjoy it. This week's book is *Dawn of the Rebels*, and I know you've read that one!"

"I—um . . ." Laura stammered, holding Evie close. Mrs. Ruiz had been gently encouraging Laura to attend Cada Palabra's fantasy book club all summer. A small part of Laura wanted to go—after all, she always had a *lot* of opinions about the books she read, and she was curious to find out what others thought.

But another, bigger part of her would rather spend two hours alone in the ice cream freezer than voluntarily talk to a roomful of people she'd never met. Even if they were talking about books.

"Actually, we're flying to Miami tomorrow," Dad said, coming to her rescue again. He slipped his phone back into his pocket and smiled at Mrs. Ruiz. "My sister's getting married this weekend, and the whole family's going to be there."

"Oh, how fun!" Mrs. Ruiz exclaimed, shifting the weight of the bag of sugar in her arms. "Well, have a wonderful time. And, Laura, maybe next weekend? *The Shadow Dagger*?"

Laura swallowed. "Maybe," she squeaked.

Mrs. Ruiz smiled. "See you then!"

She breezed out of the bodega, and Laura's shoulders slumped in relief. Dad grabbed the green folder with the inventory log and headed down the snack aisle, whistling. Laura lifted Evie higher and buried her face in the bunny's soft fur. She could feel Evie's pulse slowing, and hers slowed as well.

"Glad that's over," she whispered, and Evie's tail twitched in agreement.

No one—not Dad, not Mom, not even Melissa—truly understood what the school counselor referred to as Laura's "social anxiety." Conversations with people made her nervous. Going to new and unfamiliar places made her even more nervous. It didn't matter if the people were nice and the places were safe. That was the thing Laura couldn't seem to make her parents understand.

But Evie understood, because she was the same way.

"I wish you could come to Miami with me," Laura whispered, nuzzling Evie's head as she walked down aisle six. "Although I know you'll have fun with Amy."

Amy Rogers was a hair stylist who lived in the studio above the Rodriguezes' apartment. Whenever Laura's family went on vacation, Amy would house-sit for them, which basically meant taking care of Evie, watering the plants, and eating all of the home-made pasteles Mom left for her in the fridge.

Laura's stomach flip-flopped every time she thought about the upcoming trip. Aunt Luisa's wedding was going to be *huge*; Dad wasn't exaggerating when he said the whole family would be there—even the ones who lived in Puerto Rico. Including Uncle Hector and Aunt Ana and Laura's cousins, whom she hadn't seen in three years. Izzy, Grace, and Bianca were super nice, but they were also . . . well, a lot. At the last family reunion, they'd convinced Laura to do a choreographed dance with them in front of literally everyone. Uncle Hector had recorded the whole thing on his phone and posted it on the family reunion Facebook page he'd created. So now Laura's stiff, awkward dance moves and miserable expression lived online for everyone to see forever. (Well, everyone in her family. Thankfully, Uncle Hector had made the page private.)

When Laura thought about spending two whole days in a hotel in a new city with her cousins, suddenly book club didn't seem like such a terrible fate. What if they tried to make her dance again? Or came up with something even more humiliating? How was she going to get through this weekend without Evie?

Laura tucked Evie behind another bag of sugar,

and she could have sworn the bunny smiled in relief. She walked over to the register, then saw Dad's faraway expression and felt her stomach drop.

"What's wrong?"

Dad blinked. "What makes you think something's wrong?"

"You're just standing there," Laura said, crossing her arms. "You're not checking inventory or counting what's in the register or ordering stuff." Whenever Dad was in the bodega, he worked nonstop—there was always some task that needed to get done. On the rare occasions Laura caught him staring off into space, it meant there was a problem and he was trying to solve it.

Dad looked amused. "You know me too well."

"So what's wrong?" Laura repeated.

Sighing, Dad glanced up at the ceiling. "Before I tell you, I want you to know that Mom and I will figure out a solution. So try not to panic, okay?"

"Okay," Laura whispered, but inside she was already panicking.

"Amy just called. Her grandmother passed away."

"Oh no!"

"The funeral is this Sunday . . . in Baltimore."

"Oh . . . *oh*." Laura's eyes widened. "Amy can't watch Evie? What are we going to do? Can we take her? Do airlines allow bunnies? Is there anybody else who can house-sit? What about—"

"Laura, sweetie." Dad took Laura's hands and squeezed them tight. "Mom and I will figure this out before tomorrow. Please try not to worry about it, okay?"

Laura nodded, and Dad squeezed her hands again before letting go. *Try not to worry about it.* As if Laura controlled her anxiety instead of the other way around. Besides, their flight was tomorrow morning! How in the world were Mom and Dad going to find someone to take care of Evie before then?

2

 EVIE

Evie was totally traumatized.

To be fair, Evie was totally traumatized at least five times a day. It wasn't her fault there were so many frightening things out there! Inside the bodega, Evie felt safe . . . mostly. There were countless cozy, dark places perfect for a bunny who loved to burrow. And while people came in and out of the store, they never stayed long. Most of the time, it was just Laura and her mom and dad.

Still, dangerous things happened occasionally.

Like the time a stray dog had wandered into the bodega and chased Evie up and down the aisles, barking madly. Or the time a group of kindergartners on a field trip had come in to buy ice cream and spent fifteen minutes groping Evie's fur with their slimy, sticky fingers. Or today, with that woman who screeched so loud even though she was the one who had grabbed the bag of sugar Evie had been using for privacy, and really, wasn't Evie the one who should have been screeching?

So yes, Evie loved the bodega. But every time she heard those bells jangling, her whole body went tense. Because outside the bodega was a big and scary city, and when the door opened, a little piece of it invaded Evie's cozy world.

She breathed a sigh of relief when Laura finally brought her upstairs to the Rodriguezes' apartment for the night. When Evie wasn't in the bodega, she was in Laura's bedroom. Specifically, in the hutch— the safest, warmest, coziest place ever. Evie leaped from Laura's arms and hopped into the metal crate, going through her ritual to make sure everything was in place.

Water bottle: check.

Hay nest: check.

Pile of dandelion and cilantro: check.

Litter box: check.

Bed: check.

Evie grabbed a piece of cilantro and brought it to her bed, where she curled up in a little ball and chewed contentedly. *What an incredibly stressful day,* she thought. *Poor Laura still looks nervous. And why are her eyes so red?*

She watched as Laura moved from her closet to her dresser, pulling out clothes and folding them neatly before placing them in a flat purple bag with wheels. A suitcase, Evie realized, her pulse automatically quickening. Was Laura going away? For how long?

When Laura was finished, she left the suitcase next to her bedroom door. Evie waited anxiously, listening as Laura went into the kitchen. She heard the

Rodriguez family talking, and then she smelled the warm, spicy smell that meant Mom was cooking. She heard them chatting as they ate, and she heard the *clink-clank* sounds as they cleared the plates and washed the dishes. She heard strangers' voices and other noises that meant the television was on, and later, she heard Laura in the bathroom, brushing her teeth and getting ready for bed.

It was just like every other evening, except for that suitcase and Laura's red-rimmed eyes.

At last, Laura returned to her bedroom. She came over to the hutch, kissed her fingers, then pressed them to Evie's head.

"Good night, Evie," she whispered.

Evie relaxed slightly as Laura turned off her light and climbed into bed. Evie waited for the light from her phone to flash on, followed by the soft flutter of pages turning as she read a few chapters before going to sleep.

But the room remained dark. And Laura's breathing was off—too shallow and sniffly.

She was crying.

Evie didn't hesitate. She hurried to the door of her hutch and gently bit down on the top of the latch until it moved down just a little bit. Then she stuck her paw between the bars, pressed the button, and the door sprang open.

Scampering across the room, Evie leaped up into Laura's bed and crawled under the blankets. Laura let out a half sob, half giggle as Evie squirmed beneath her arm and curled up next to her side.

"Is that door broken again?" she whispered, stroking Evie between the ears.

Evie smiled to herself. The door was super easy to open. She just never opened it unless it was an emergency.

After several minutes, Laura's breathing deepened. Evie's eyelids began to droop, and she snuggled closer to Laura. *Everything's fine*, Evie told herself. *There's nothing to worry about.*

She drifted off to sleep, trying not to think about the suitcase still sitting next to the door.

* * *

Laura's alarm blared before the sun was even up. Evie jumped so high, she hit the roof of her hutch.

She scrambled back onto her bed, watching as Laura sat up and stretched. Something wasn't right. Laura only set her alarm when she had school, and she was on summer break. Plus, she never woke up when it was still dark outside, not even for school!

Evie's ears twitched as she listened to Laura and her parents move around the apartment, banging around the kitchen and running water in the bathroom. When Laura returned to her bedroom with her mom, Evie's relief lasted only a moment.

"I know Mrs. Vanderwaal takes care of lots of cats, but are you sure she can take care of a bunny?" Laura's eyes were pink and watery as she gazed at Evie.

Mom smiled gently as she walked over to Evie's hutch carrying a blanket. "Of course she can, sweetie. Mrs. Vanderwaal is one of the most experienced volunteers at the shelter. I promise, Evie will be just fine."

With that, Mom covered Evie's hutch with the blanket, and everything went dark.

Normally, Evie loved the darkness. But then something unthinkably horrific happened.

Her hutch started to move!

Evie crammed herself into a corner, her heart hammering out of control. What in the world was going on?

"Can't I take her out and hold her in my lap?" Laura's voice was all wobbly and cracked.

"Pets on the train have to be in crates, hon," Mom replied lightly, and Evie realized she was carrying the hutch. "Subway rules. Besides, I think Evie will be less scared in here!"

Evie's ears flattened against her head. What was a subway? It sounded terrifying!

She couldn't see anything, but her nose and ears told her that Mom were taking her hutch out of Laura's bedroom. Then out of the apartment. Then out of the bodega!

The next half hour was a total nightmare.

Every muscle in Evie's little body was tense as she listened to roars and squeals and tinny voices announcing things like *"Next stop, 72nd Street!"* and other terrifying sounds. But at least Laura and Mom were there—Evie could smell them, and she could hear them talking.

At last, Mom picked up the hutch again. Evie sniffed and sniffed, hoping to catch the familiar scent of the bodega. But these smells were all completely unfamiliar.

"Wow, fancy building," Laura said. "Which button should I push?"

"Four," Mom replied.

Evie froze as the whole world seemed to lurch up. Several seconds later, the motion stopped abruptly. The hutch jostled as Mom carried the crate a few steps, and then: *knock-knock-knock!*

"Adriana! Come on in!" said a warm, kind voice.

"Thank you so much for doing this, Blair," Mom replied, stepping forward with the hutch. "I really appreciate it."

She set the hutch down gently, and a moment later, the blanket vanished. Evie went completely, perfectly still. Even her heart seemed to freeze in her chest.

This place was the exact opposite of the Rodriguezes' apartment. Everything was bright white—the floors, the walls, the furniture—and it smelled like fake lemons.

I'm not in Harlem anymore, Evie thought in horror.

A woman with yellow hair and a slightly crooked nose beamed down at Evie. "Well, she's just the cutest thing!" she exclaimed. "I bet she and Wentworth are going to be best friends."

What was a Wentworth? Evie didn't know how much more of this she could take. She gazed at Laura, silently pleading with her to take Evie back to the bodega.

"Evie's pretty shy," Mom said, placing her hand on Laura's shoulder. "But I'm sure she'll adjust in no time. Right, hon?"

Laura swallowed and nodded. "Thank you for watching her, Mrs. Vanderwaal."

Mrs. Vanderwaal waved a hand dismissively. "Oh, please, it's my pleasure! Can I get you two anything to drink? Coffee, juice . . ."

"Oh, thank you, but we have a plane to catch," Mom replied, already moving toward the door.

"Of course, of course!" Mrs. Vanderwaal followed her, but Laura moved closer to the hutch. She knelt down, opened the door, and grazed the top of Evie's head with her fingers. For a brief moment, Evie's pulse slowed, and she relaxed a tiny bit. So she wasn't in the bodega. But as long as Laura was here, everything would be okay.

"Be good, okay?" Laura whispered. "I love you, Evie."

What?!

Evie stared in disbelief as Laura stood up and walked over to join her mother. They said goodbye to Mrs. Vanderwaal, who waved and closed the door behind them.

Laura was gone.

Laura had *left* her.

Mrs. Vanderwaal disappeared, then reappeared a moment later with a bundle of leafy greens. "Fresh arugula," she said, setting it inside Evie's hutch. "I'll leave this door open so you can explore, okay?"

She headed off to another room. Evie sniffed tentatively at the arugula. It smelled nice and peppery, but she was far too stressed to eat at the moment. Why had Laura been crying? Why had she brought Evie here? When was she coming back?

Was she coming back?

Evie needed a dark, cozy place to burrow so she could think clearly. Normally, her hutch would be perfect—but out of Laura's room, in this blindingly white place with its weird fake lemon smell, it didn't feel cozy at all. Evie's eyes darted around, taking in her surroundings. Behind the sofa? Nope, too close to the wall. Under the table? Nope, the top was glass so it wasn't dark under there. What about the shelves? Nope, there was hardly anything on them—just a few colorful bowls and bottles. Laura's shelves were crammed with books, and the bodega shelves were crammed with food and all kinds of things. *What was the point of a shelf if you weren't going to cram a bunch of stuff on it?* Evie wondered anxiously.

Then her gaze fell on a door. It was barely open, enough for Evie to see that inside was totally, blissfully dark.

Cautiously, Evie crept out of her hutch. She cast one more glance around the empty room, then scurried across the floor as fast as she could.

Inside, Evie quickly took stock of her surroundings. It was very small—a closet, she reasoned, because there was a pair of rain boots just inside the door, and the Rodriguez family kept their boots in a closet. But other than the boots and a few coats hanging above Evie, Mrs. Vanderwaal's closet was empty.

At last, Evie allowed herself to let out a breath and relax.

"Well, hello there."

"Ahhh!" Evie jumped straight up, brushing against the bottom of a coat. She landed with a *thud*, then backed herself into a corner. "Who said that?"

"Over here, darling." In the shadows, Evie could just make out a pair of glowing eyes as a creature emerged from behind the boots. He sat primly near the door, and Evie stared in astonishment. The creature was much larger than her, although a lot of his size was due to the fluffiness of his white fur. His ears were much shorter than hers, but his tail was much longer.

Evie was too frightened to speak. Fortunately, the creature didn't seem to mind.

"My name is Wentworth." His magnificent whiskers twitched as he spoke. "Welcome to my home. I'm sure you'll be quite comfortable here until arrangements have been made with your new family. Now, if you'll follow me, I'll give you the tour."

All of this was delivered in a long, monotonous drawl, as if Wentworth had given this speech a hundred times. He slipped out of the closet. When

Evie didn't follow, he butted the door so that it swung open wider.

"Well, what are you—oh my." Wentworth blinked. "You aren't a cat, are you?"

"I'm a bunny," she managed to squeak. "Are *you* a cat?"

"Am I a cat?" Wentworth's massive, fluffy tail swooshed through the air in a grand arc. "Darling, I am a Persian cat, the most beautiful and intelligent of all cats and, indeed, all animals. Do you have a name?"

"E-Evie. What did you mean about a new family?" Evie blurted out. "I already have a family! I have Laura."

"Was Laura the one who brought you here?" Wentworth asked, and Evie nodded frantically. "Then she is not your family anymore."

Evie stopped breathing. "What?"

"You're a foster pet now, darling," Wentworth explained, lazily cleaning his paw. "Mrs. Vanderwaal is a wonderful foster mom, so don't fret. You'll be quite comfortable here until you're adopted. Now, let's get on with the tour—we have some ground rules to cover."

He sashayed across the room, but Evie didn't move. She just stared as his swishing tail, trying to grasp what Wentworth had just told her.

Laura wasn't coming back.

Ever.

3

 BART

Most street dogs knew how to survive. Bartholomew Porpington III knew how to *thrive*.

He trotted toward the old bridge that crossed the pond, stopping by the hot dog vendor who always "accidentally" dropped a wiener when a dog happened to walk past. The vendor winked at Bart, who wagged gratefully as he gobbled down the treat.

"Aw, what a cute doggie!" a little girl exclaimed. "Where's his owner, Mommy?"

Far away from here, thank goodness. Bart gave the

girl's hand a polite kiss—he might be a stray, but he was still a gentledog. All Shiba Inus were.

After allowing the girl to pat him twice on the head, Bart headed across the bridge. The sun was out, the sky was blue, and Central Park was crowded with people. Some were walking, some were running, and some were cycling, skateboarding, roller-skating, scootering, and all the other funny things humans did by strapping wheels onto themselves.

Of course, the park was crowded with dogs, too.

"Bart! Bart! Bart-Bart-Bart!"

"Hey, Spark!" Bart slowed as the tiny pug lunged toward him, straining against his leash. Spark's owner, Zane, a bearded man who always wore flannel shirts even in the middle of summer, kept his eyes on his phone screen.

"We're going to the dog park and Zane has a ball and we're gonna play fetch! Can you believe it?" Spark spun in a circle until his leash wrapped around his back legs.

Bart tilted his head as Spark untangled himself.

"Well, yes. You go to the dog park to play fetch every morning, don't you?"

"We *do*!" Spark wagged not just his tail, but his entire rear end. "Wanna come?"

"Nah, I'm running late for work. Have fun!"

"See ya!" Spark lurched forward, half dragging Zane, who still kept his eyes fixed on his phone. "Fetch-fetch-fetch-fetch-fetch . . ."

Bart tried not to roll his eyes as he continued across the bridge. He used to enjoy going to the dog park, too. But now it made him feel sad—and maybe a tiny bit superior—to see how excited other dogs became the moment their owners unhooked their leashes and set them free. Well, free within the fences surrounding the dog park. Bart rarely visited his old stomping grounds anymore. Why would he? All of Manhattan was his off-leash dog park! Best of all, it was filled with buskers: people who played music or danced or did other entertaining things for money. And lots of them were happy to have a talented pup like Bart join in their act.

As Bart ambled off the bridge, he spotted his first appointment: the guitarist with the spiky hair who played weird, sad remixes of Taylor Swift songs—and kept a bag of Snausages in his guitar case. Bart made his way through the small crowd gathered around the guitarist, then snatched the upside-down fedora lying next to the case in his teeth. The guitarist grinned as Bart moved from one person to the next, gazing up at them with his best puppy-dog eyes. Sure enough, every single one of them laughed and opened their wallets.

When Bart deposited the fedora filled with bills and coins next to the case, the guitarist winked at him.

"Help yourself, buddy!"

Eagerly, Bart dove into the case, grabbed as many Snausages as his mouth could hold, then raced off to his next appointment.

Over by the carousel, Holly the Hula-Hoop Queen already had a pretty big crowd. She stood on an overturned crate, and Bart counted four—no, five—hoops already circling her arms, waist, legs, and even her neck! Holly's act was amazing, but Bart always helped her take it to the next level.

Several onlookers cried out in surprise as the orange-and-white dog leaped into the act. Beaming, Holly kept the hoops around her waist and left leg going while holding out another hoop in her right hand. Bart hopped through easily, then spun around just as she raised the hoop higher. Another flawless jump, and now more people were gathering, taking videos and photos on their phones. Holly picked up speed, moving hoops from her arms to her legs to her waist as if by magic, always holding one out for Bart to jump through.

Bart reveled in the applause. It was times like this that he missed being a show dog. Really, it would have been the perfect life—fame, fortune, fun obstacle courses. But his former owner, the coldhearted Bitsy DuPont, had turned what should've been a dream job into a total nightmare.

Once Holly had given Bart his usual payment

(apple slices and a bowl of fresh water), he headed toward the southwest corner of Central Park. It was Friday, which meant the big group of hip-hop dancers in Columbus Circle would be getting a huge crowd. Last time Bart had hopped in on their routine, one of the dancers had given him an entire hamburger!

Bart could already hear the *thump-thump-thump* of the music. But right before he reached the southwest exit, he saw something that stopped him in his tracks.

There was a new busker! Bart wagged his tail excitedly, hurrying closer to get a good look. An older man with a wispy gray beard was playing the accordion with surprising vigor. He had tiny cymbals tied to one ankle and a little tambourine around the other, so they went *crash-jingle-crash-jingle* as he stomped out a beat. The accordionist had a pretty decent crowd . . . but was he a dog person? Not all buskers appreciated Bart, as he'd learned when a man covered in spray paint and pretending to be a statue had tried to kick him when Bart licked his leg. (Bart hadn't even been trying to get in on the act—he just wanted to make sure the frozen man was okay!)

Would the accordionist appreciate Bart, or try to kick him?

Only one way to find out, Bart thought.

This was his most difficult trick, the one that Bart pulled out to win over the snootiest dog-show judges. He crept to the front of the crowd, who'd started clapping in time with the song. And then Bart stood on his hind legs and strode out in front of the accordionist.

Well, maybe *strode* wasn't the right word. More like *hopped*. Still, the crowd ate it up! Bart's tongue lolled as he swayed and dipped, twirled and bobbed, all on his hind legs. The accordionist laughed and picked up the tempo, and Bart did his best to keep up. He did a hop to the left, then a twist, then—

Uh-oh.

Bart froze, locking eyes with a familiar young

man in the crowd. He carried a long pole with a steel loop at the end, and he wore a dark shirt with white letters on the front pocket. Bart knew that uniform.

This guy was a dogcatcher, and he was staring right at Bart.

Thanks to Bart's extra-refined manners and beautiful coat, he didn't *look* like a street dog. The only problem was that he didn't have a collar anymore. Bart tore his gaze away from the dogcatcher and continued dancing. Usually, he'd trot over to the nearest humans who looked dog friendly and pretend to be their pet until the dogcatcher had moved on. Right now, he'd have to hope this guy thought he was the accordionist's pet.

When the song ended, the crowd burst into cheers. Bart fell back to all fours, tired but happy, and looked hopefully at the accordionist as people crowded around his case, dropping in bills and coins. The accordionist held out his hand to Bart and smiled.

"Come here, boy!"

Bart let out a short bark and hurried over. Together, they walked over to the hot dog cart. Bart started to drool . . . but then the accordionist passed the cart, and Bart's head drooped.

"Here we are. Two, please!"

Bart looked up, and suddenly, he wanted to dance on his hind legs again. The accordionist had stopped in front of a vendor on the other side of the hot dog cart. Beneath a red-and-yellow umbrella, the vendor was holding out two sticks, each loaded with cubes of steak.

Street meat!

"Arf! Arf!" Bart spun in a circle, unable to help himself. Street meat was his *favorite* food! The accordionist handed him a stick, and Bart just barely remembered his manners, giving the man's hand a quick lick before grabbing the stick and scurrying over to a nearby bench to devour it.

He was so lost in his joy over the street meat that he didn't realize the accordionist was talking to someone until it was too late.

"That was really something, Clyde!"

"Oh, hey there, Jeff!" the accordionist said, his mouth full. "Didn't see you watching."

"Great dog you've got there. How long have you had him?"

"Oh, he's not mine! I think he's a stray, actually."

Oh no.

Gulping the last cube of street meat down whole, Bart dropped the stick. He turned slowly, and his stomach flip-flopped.

The dogcatcher—Jeff—was staring right at him.

There was only one thing to do: Bart fled the park, racing into Columbus Circle as fast as he could, Jeff running and shouting behind him.

4

 LAURA

LaGuardia Airport was more crowded than the 1 train at rush hour, and that was saying something. Laura and her parents hurried through the terminal, passing a bookstore, a clothing boutique, and a Starbucks with a line of grumpy-looking travelers that extended from Gate C9 to C14. When they passed a Shake Shack, Laura inhaled deeply. Normally, the smell of cheeseburgers and fries—and just the idea of a black-and-white custard shake—would make her stomach rumble with hunger. But right now, Laura's stomach was too busy tying itself up in a million knots to notice.

Flying was the *worst*. Getting through security was always so stressful, with everyone in a mad dash to take the shoes off their feet and the laptops out of their bags and spreading all their belongings out in bins, only to hurriedly put it all back together again while the conveyor belt kept moving and people kept shoving and grumbling. Then there was the matter of finding the right gate, which wasn't always as easy as it should be, especially because sometimes airlines just randomly changed gates, and what if you had to run to another terminal and missed your flight?

But even if you made your flight, Laura thought miserably, *the stress didn't end there.* She was dreading the idea of sitting in a cramped seat for the next three hours. Once, she'd ended up in a seat several rows away from her parents. A *middle* seat. Between *strangers.* The woman in the window seat had slept the whole flight, but the one in the aisle seat had been . . . chatty. Laura shuddered at the memory. Trapped in a flying tube with a stranger who seemed to think the fact that Laura was holding a book meant she wanted to talk about her favorite books with a person she didn't even know rather than actually *read her book.*

But this time, Laura was sitting in the same row as her parents. She'd triple-checked their tickets to be sure. And she checked one more time when they reached their gate and joined the boarding line.

"Doing okay, hon?" Mom asked, glancing over her shoulder. She was slightly out of breath, and her thick dark bangs were damp with sweat. It was almost a hundred degrees outside, the kind of summer day in New York City that went to battle with air-conditioning and won.

"Yeah," Laura replied. *Not at all,* she thought miserably. Because on top of all of this—the noisy airport, the security lines, and the crowded plane she was about to board—Laura couldn't stop thinking about Evie. Her poor little bunny had looked so confused, cowering in her crate in Mrs. Vanderwaal's apartment. The bodega and the Rodriguezes' apartment had been Evie's whole world; she'd never even been in Amy's apartment upstairs! And Laura had just dragged her all the way across Manhattan and dumped her with a stranger.

The guilt was even worse than the anxiety. Laura's throat tightened every time she pictured Evie. It didn't matter that Mrs. Vanderwaal was super nice, and that she volunteered at the animal shelter with Mom, and that her apartment was really big and fancy. She was a stranger. And that meant Evie was going to be miserable.

The moment Laura took her seat—by the window, with Mom and Dad safely next to her—she pulled out her phone and opened the Photos app. She scrolled through her pictures of Evie, and suddenly her eyes felt hot and itchy.

"Oooh, look at all these movies!" Dad said, reaching over to press the buttons on the screen in front of Laura. "You brought your earphones, right?"

Laura nodded, fishing them out of her pocket. "I'm just going to read, though."

"Sure, sweetie." Dad smiled at her.

Laura pulled out her book—*The Shadow Dagger,* which she was reading because it sounded good and *not* because it was next week's book club pick at Cada Palabra—and slid out her bookmark. Chapter five had ended with a serious cliff-hanger, but Laura read the first paragraph of the next chapter at least ten times without comprehending a word. Her mind kept wandering back to Evie.

Sighing, Laura closed the book and slid it into the pocket of the seat in front of her. As the plane pulled away from the gate, she took out her phone and opened Twitter. Her thumbs moved quickly over the screen as she typed:

@JALBodegaBunny: First time away from home! I hope my babysitter has lots of raspberries in the fridge. #bunnycation

Laura added a photo of Evie happily gnawing on a raspberry before sending the tweet. Then she closed the app and set her phone to airplane mode.

"She's going to be just fine, hon."

Startled, Laura glanced up and realized Dad and

Mom were both watching her. She smiled, squeezing her hands in her lap.

"Yeah, I know."

The plane turned slowly, heading for the runway. Laura glanced at her book, but she knew she'd never be able to focus. She tapped Movies on the screen, then stopped after just one swipe.

"Hey, look!" Laura found herself grinning. "Remember this one?"

Dad let out a good-natured groan. *"Apple's Amazing Adventure.* Oh, that brings back memories."

"I still hear that theme song in my dreams," Mom added wryly.

"I think you mean nightmares," Dad said, chuckling when Laura elbowed him.

Apple's Amazing Adventure had come out when Laura was in second grade, and she had been *obsessed.* This was before the Rodriguezes adopted Evie, and Laura had wanted a pet more than anything. So the story of Apple, a hamster who got lost when her family moved to a new city, hit her right in the heart. She had every line memorized. Her parents did, too.

"Oh no, you're not seriously watching it, are you?" Mom exclaimed when Laura plugged her earphones in. Laura responded by sticking her tongue out, and Dad laughed.

"Just as long as *we* don't have to watch it."

The plane suddenly picked up speed, and Laura lowered her hand and stared out the window. This was the one thing about flying she loved—the actual *flying*. Dad leaned closer, and they both gazed out the window as the plane left the ground.

The tarmac fell away, and Laura held her breath as they rose higher and higher. Soon she could see the whole airport, and then the rows of houses in Queens, the river . . . and there was Manhattan, a long, surprisingly small island covered in buildings. Laura spotted the green patch in the middle that she knew was Central Park, and she pressed her fingers to the window.

JAL Corner Deli was north of the park. But right

now, Evie was south of the park, all the way down by Columbus Circle. And she was getting farther and farther away by the second.

Dad placed his hand on Laura's arm. "Evie's amazing adventure is about to begin," he joked. "She's going to have a blast with Mrs. Vanderwaal!"

Laura tried to smile. "She'll probably just hide in the closet the whole time."

Dad laughed, and Laura turned her attention back to the window. But the plane had turned, and all she could see now was an endless blue sky dotted with fluffy white clouds.

Her stomach clenched again as she remembered where she was going. Miami. Wedding. Cousins. Pushy, chatty, *dancing* cousins.

At least Evie was still in New York. Laura was the one heading off on an adventure—but she wasn't sure it would be amazing.

5

 EVIE

"And this is the guest bathroom. You'll notice the marble tile, of course—it's the coolest surface in the house, perfect for lounging on hot days like today. As a matter of fact, that's what I was doing before your arrival interrupted my nap. But it's my pleasure to give our newcomers a tour, darling. Now, if you'll follow me . . ."

Wentworth continued rambling on in his drawling voice as he swished from room to room, Evie trailing miserably behind him. She barely took in a word he said, although she did get the sense that she was supposed to be very impressed by Mrs. Vanderwaal's apartment. True, it was enormous, and Evie knew that was important to humans— Laura's parents would occasionally talk about how nice it would be to have a bigger place. But for bunnies, all that extra space was a nightmare. Evie would never want a bigger crate, for example. What if it was big enough for another animal to hide in? She would never feel safe!

"And *this*," Wentworth said grandly, swiveling around to face Evie, "is the highlight of our little tour—my pavilion."

He stepped aside, and Evie felt her ears flatten against her head. "Oh . . . my" was all she managed to say.

They stood in the doorway of what was either a very small room or a very large closet. It was completely empty save for a ridiculously ornate cat bed. Or at least Evie thought it was a bed. The thing—a *pavilion*, Wentworth had called it—had four posts and a little roof, all made from dark polished wood carved into smooth curves. At the top sat what looked almost like a golden egg covered in green and purple jewels. Red velvet curtains parted to reveal what looked like a plush bed inside.

"Fabulous, isn't it?" Wentworth crooned. "Just wait till you see the inside."

He leaped gracefully through the curtains, and after a moment's hesitation, Evie poked her head inside. Her eyes widened, and for a brief moment, she almost managed to forget about Laura abandoning her.

"What *is* all this stuff?"

The far left corner of the bed was covered in . . . well, *trash* wasn't the right word. Evie had watched Laura take out the bodega's trash enough to know what that looked like: food scraps, empty bottles, used paper towels. Here in Wentworth's pavilion, Evie saw a plum-purple high-heel shoe streaked with dirt, a pearl brooch in the shape of an owl, an iPhone in a glittery silver case, and when her gaze fell on what looked like a half-eaten pigeon wing, Evie quickly looked away.

"These are my treasures." Wentworth sat primly in the opposite corner, grooming his paw. "My collection. I fancy myself a bit of an explorer, you see. You'd be amazed at what you can find out there on the streets of Manhattan. That's a Jimmy Choo, right there!" His tail flicked in the direction of the plum-purple shoe.

Evie scrunched her nose. "You named it?"

For some reason, this made Wentworth chuckle. "Oh, you're a funny little thing, aren't you? Now, I know what you're thinking, and yes, Mrs. Vanderwaal buys me plenty of toys. This collection of mine is our little secret, okay, sweetheart? And don't worry, she always spoils the other animals rotten, too. In fact, I'm absolutely certain that she'll take you to Priscilla's Pampered Pets soon enough."

"Priscilla?" Evie repeated numbly.

"Oh, just you wait," Wentworth said eagerly. "It's this wonderful boutique shop in the Upper East Side.

That's where she bought this pavilion, and all my other things as well! Trips there are complete bliss, Evie, you'll see. The manager lavishes caviar and sushi on you until you're so full you can barely—"

"I don't want to go to Priscilla's!" The words spilled out before Evie could stop herself. She was shaking all over. Wentworth gaped at her, his green eyes unblinking.

"But, Evie, it's—"

"I'm sorry, I don't mean to be rude, but the thing is, I have a family and a home already," Evie said quickly. "Laura's coming back for me. She would never just leave me here."

Wentworth let out a gusty sigh. "Oh, my dear sweet Evie," he said, as if they'd been friends for years. "I've seen this all too many times. Once, Mrs. Vanderwaal brought home a cat named Gus— dreadful name, breath like rotten fish, but not a bad sort, overall. He'd been with his owners for nearly ten years. Then they moved into a building that didn't allow pets, and"—Wentworth flicked his paw—"so long, Gus. It took him weeks to finally understand they weren't coming back for him."

"That's different," Evie said, her heart flipping over at the thought. "*Laura's* different."

Wentworth was quiet for a moment, regarding her with those green eyes. "And yet," he said finally, "here you are."

Evie's mouth opened, then closed. She began to quiver. She didn't want to live in this too-clean apartment with Wentworth and Jimmy Shoe. She didn't want a brand-new family. She wanted Laura! She wanted the bodega!

Panic seized her, and before Evie knew it, she was scurrying out of the pavilion. She scooted out into the hall, through the living room, up the couch, onto the windowsill, which was cracked open . . . and there she stopped, her breaths coming in frantic bursts as her eyes took in the fire escape, four flights of rickety metal steps that led to the bustling city streets far below.

Deep down, Evie knew that unless she wanted to

submit to her fate, her only choice was to find her way back to JAL Corner Deli all by herself. But just looking at the chaos of cars and people was making her heart race. Was she really brave enough to wander those streets alone? And even if she managed to survive, how would she ever find her way home?

"Well, if you're so determined to prove me wrong . . . the fire escape's not your only option, you know."

Spinning around, Evie saw Wentworth sprawled across the smooth white floor, his tail flicking from left to right and back again. He looked almost amused.

"What do you mean?" Evie asked cautiously.

"I mean, I'm well-practiced at sneaking out," Wentworth told her. "The fire escape isn't for the faint of heart, and you, honey, are the faintest heart I've ever met. But not to worry. There's an easier way." He nodded toward the front door. "The elevator."

Evie blinked. "That little room with the buttons? I wouldn't even be able to—"

"Just listen," Wentworth interrupted smoothly. "Play it right, and you don't have to push a single button. See, when the elevator isn't in use, it rests on the first level. So all you have to do is wait by the front door and, when Mrs. Vanderwaal gets home, dart outside and get on that elevator before the doors close. It'll take you down, the doors open, and voilà. All you have to do is cross the lobby unseen—very easy, as the doorman is always playing games on his phone—and you're outside!"

For a half second, Evie thought that didn't sound too bad. Then she remembered what waited outside: cars and trucks and dogs and people in a big hurry and probably a hundred other horrors Evie couldn't even imagine.

"I can't," she whispered, her whiskers drooping. "I just can't do it."

Wentworth made a soft, sympathetic sound. Or maybe it was a purr—he *was* rubbing his back end on the couch. Evie turned and gazed at her crate on the other side of the room. Maybe she should just stay here for a while and hope that Laura came back for her. After all, Mrs. Vanderwaal's place wasn't so bad, was it? She was very friendly, and that arugula *had* smelled delicious. Her apartment might be too big, but it was very quiet, which Evie appreciated.

She took a tentative hop toward her crate, her mind just about made up. Then the front door swung open, and a familiar sound filled the apartment. A sound Evie knew all too well thanks to countless days spent in the bodega.

The ear-piercing squeals of small children.

With a yowl, Wentworth leaped a foot into the air. "Every cat for himself!" he cried before clambering up the couch. To Evie's astonishment, he somehow managed to slither through the crack in the windowsill like a fluffy snake, then scrambled down the fire escape.

Heart in her throat, Evie whirled back around to face the door. Mrs. Vanderwaal was crouching in the entrance, helping a grubby-cheeked blond boy take off his sandals. Next to him, a woman who looked like a slightly younger Mrs. Vanderwaal was setting a few duffel bags down, while a girl with pigtails clutching a gigantic lollipop gazed around the living room. Her eyes fell on Evie, and she gasped so hard she almost swallowed the sucker whole.

"Auntie Blair, Auntie Blair! Did you get a *bunny*?"

Run! Evie's mind screamed, but every one of her tiny muscles had seized up in fear. She cowered and squeezed her eyes shut as the boy and girl toddled over to her as fast as their chubby legs could carry them.

And then their sticky hands were pawing at her, pulling out little tufts of fur, yanking on her ears and tail. In the background, Evie heard Mrs. Vanderwaal saying something about needing to "play gently," but like most kids, these two didn't seem to know what *gentle* meant. Evie shook as a finger jabbed her in the eye, and she felt a hard tugging on her side.

"My sucker!" the little girl wailed. Evie opened one eye in a squint and saw that the slimy lollipop was stuck to her back end. "Mommy, the bunny stole my sucker!"

"Annabelle, honestly," the girl's mother chided as she hurried over. "Blair, I'm so sorry. They aren't used to having pets around . . ."

"Don't worry about it!" Mrs. Vanderwaal said brightly. "We have all weekend to learn how to play nicely with the bunny." She knelt down and carefully peeled the lollipop from Evie's fur, causing Evie to cringe. Mrs. Vanderwaal gave her a little scratch behind the ears. "Now, Annabanana, let's see if we can find you a non-furry treat, shall we?"

Annabelle giggled, and she and her brother scurried after Mrs. Vanderwaal as she headed into the kitchen. Their mother gave Evie a pat on the head, then picked up the duffel bags and headed down the hall.

Evie trembled. Those awful children were staying the whole weekend? Well, that changed everything. The streets of Manhattan were nothing compared to the horror of toddlers.

Mrs. Vanderwaal had left the front door wide open. Through it, Evie could see the elevator, but the doors were closed. Her heart pitter-pattered against her ribs. Wentworth said the elevator automatically went down to the first floor. But Evie had missed her chance.

Ding!

Like magic, the elevator doors slid open. A couple strolled out hand in hand, laughing at something on the man's phone. As they disappeared down the hall, the doors began to close.

It was now or never.

Suddenly, Evie bolted across the living room before she had time to second-guess herself. She just barely managed to squeeze through the doors in time. The elevator was mercifully empty, and Evie allowed herself a small moment of triumph. She'd done it! Now the elevator would take her down to the lobby.

Except . . .

Evie swallowed hard as the elevator began to

move. *Up.* She gazed at the row of buttons and saw the one at the very top was glowing.

"No, no, no, no, no!" Evie cowered in the corner as the elevator rose higher and higher. Had Wentworth lied to her? But why would he do that?

When the doors slid open, Evie was greeted with a sight almost as terrifying as sticky-handed toddlers.

A party.

Through a sea of swimsuits and bare legs, Evie spotted blue sky and a swimming pool. For a moment, her heart leaped—maybe she had gone down to the first floor after all! Then she saw the tops of other buildings spread out in all directions and realized she was on the roof.

"So then I told her she was being ridiculous, I mean, it's not her fault her manager can't figure out how to—*omigod!*"

A woman wearing a bright pink bathing suit that matched her spiky hair let out a squeal when she saw Evie. A man in sunglasses who had taken a step onto the elevator glanced down, then stumbled backward like Evie was a menacing monster instead of a terrified bunny. He bumped into two other guys, who bumped into a woman carrying a tray of drinks, which flew into the air—

CRASH!

Glasses smashed on the floor, and suddenly everyone was in a panic. Evie darted out of the elevator to more screams and shrieks, weaving between sunscreen-slathered legs and hopping over flip-flops, scurrying under lounge chairs and around table legs. Instinctively, she headed for the far corner of the roof, far away from the pool and the swimmers and the people milling around, trying to figure out what all the hubbub was over by the elevator. Evie leaped up onto a table, then again onto a ledge, and felt a wave of dizziness wash over her.

It was the same view she'd had from Mrs. Vanderwaal's window, only now Evie was much, *much* higher. The black metal stairs of the fire escape zigzagged all the way down to the street, which was just as crowded and scary as ever. In fact, Evie could see even more streets from this height, each more frightening than the last. But there, just a few blocks away . . . a *park*!

Evie gazed longingly at all the trees. There would be so many quiet places for a bunny to burrow in the park. Of course, first she had to actually get there.

Quivering, Evie glanced back at the pool party. In front of the elevator, people were still picking themselves up and helping clean up all the broken glass. If Evie wanted to get to that park, she only had one option.

Steeling herself, Evie jumped off the ledge and onto the steel grate platform. She gazed down at what looked like thousands of steps below her. "One at a time," Evie told herself, and hopped down onto the first step.

6

 **BART**

Four years of agility course training—jumping through hoops, weaving around tightly packed poles, scrambling through tunnels, and racing up ramps—had earned Bart no fewer than six Best in Show medals. But now it was *really* paying off.

Tongue lolling, Bart chanced a glance behind him as he dodged picnickers and sunbathers lounging on the grass. Jeff the dogcatcher didn't stand a chance. He wasn't giving up, though, and Bart had to admit, the guy was pretty quick on his feet.

Just not quick enough, Bart thought smugly as the

exit on the southwest side of the park came into view. The *thump-thump* music of the hip-hop dancers in Columbus Circle was louder now, but Bart couldn't risk exposing himself to more attention with Jeff hot on his heels. Bart blasted out of the park and veered hard to the right, speeding around the circle until he spotted a couple standing in front of an ice cream cart. As they stepped away, each holding a cone, Bart slowed to a trot right behind them. He followed them nearly two blocks, checking every few seconds to make sure Jeff was nowhere in sight. Finally, the couple wandered into a bookstore, and Bart sat down near the entrance to catch his breath.

His triumph only lasted a few seconds. It wasn't just that Jeff had gotten a good look at him. The dogcatcher had seen what Bart was doing: busking. All he had to do now was hide out and watch the buskers every day until Bart showed up. Bart had outrun Jeff today, but eventually the pup's luck would run out. The dogcatcher's steel loop would slide around his neck, and *BOOM*. Hello, shelter. Goodbye, freedom.

"Come on, Pickles. I said *come on!*" Across the street, a girl carrying at least half a dozen grocery bags in one hand tugged impatiently at a leash with her other hand. At the end of the leash, a tiny shih tzu sniffed around a tree, blissfully unaware of her owner's frustration. Bart couldn't help but cringe as the girl gave a firm yank, and Pickles nearly toppled over. She righted herself immediately and trotted along at her owner's side, the tags on her collar glinting in the sun.

A collar. That would solve all Bart's problems. If he was wearing a collar, no one would think he was a stray. But how could he get one?

Bart gazed at the building across the street, so lost in thought that at first he didn't see the movement. Then his instincts kicked in, and his fur rose before he even realized what he was looking at.

Something small and fuzzy was scrambling down the building's fire escape, one step at a time. A cat?

No, those ears were so long, and that tail was just a fluffy stub. Bart tilted his head curiously. It almost looked like . . . no, it couldn't be.

But it was—it *was* a bunny!

Bart watched as the bunny crouched on the last step of the fire escape, a good ten feet from the ground. Even from this far away, he could tell the poor thing was vibrating with fear. Bart could almost sense the furry creature's thoughts: It was too far to jump but climbing back up was just as intimidating. Was the bunny a runaway pet, like Bart? Escaping a miserable life and making a bid for freedom?

He was already on his feet, trying to think of a way to help—but then a vendor pushing a snow cone cart with a gigantic umbrella passed right underneath the fire escape.

Bart knew what the bunny would do a split second before she did it. "Attagirl!" he said, feeling a surge of admiration as the bunny leaped. She slid down the umbrella and landed nimbly on the concrete, and the vendor's eyes widened in horror.

"Rat!" he bellowed.

Wuh-oh, thought Bart as several passersby turned to see what all the commotion was about. The bunny went into panic mode, darting this way and that as people screamed and jumped out of her way. For a moment, Bart was amused.

Until the bunny sprinted into the street.

"Stop!" Bart lunged forward, barking frantically. Horns honked, tires squealed, people shrieked. Soon, every car on the street was at a standstill.

Bart dodged around a truck, his heart racing a mile a minute. Was he too late? Then he spotted her—a tiny gray bunny, curled up right behind the truck's front tire and shaking so hard she was almost a blur.

"This isn't safe!" he called. "Follow me!"

The bunny didn't respond, just continued to tremble. Bart had the impression that she was so shocked, she couldn't even hear him. It didn't help that up and down the street, people were yelling and shouting up a storm. The driver of the truck, a man with a long face and a longer frown, leaned out of his window.

"Hey, what's the holdup? Let's *go!*"

He revved his engine, and the truck shifted forward half an inch. The bunny let out a surprised squeak.

"You're going to get run over if you don't follow me *now!*" Bart shouted, and at last, she seemed to hear him. She crept out from behind the tire, and Bart took a few steps back, heading for the sidewalk.

"There you go, just a few more steps . . ."

"Whoa, what happened out here?" someone said. Bart glanced behind him and saw the couple he'd followed standing just outside the bookstore. A woman in a baseball cap pointed down the street.

"Not sure, but it looks like traffic's jammed all the way around Columbus Circle!"

By now, everyone on the sidewalk had come to a halt. Bart stood stiffly on the curb, watching the bunny creep closer and closer. She seemed terrified of the attention, when she should have been terrified of all the angry drivers trying to edge their cars forward to see what was going on.

"You're almost there," Bart said, keeping his eyes locked on hers. "Just a few more steps—there!"

"Oh my gosh, it's a bunny!"

Bart glanced up as the woman in the baseball cap whipped out her phone. She wasn't the only one; several people, including the driver of the truck, were taking photos and videos. Bart saw the bunny's ears flatten as all of those phones were suddenly aimed at her.

"Come with me!" he said, and this time, the bunny didn't hesitate. They sprinted down the sidewalk together, leaving the chaos of Columbus Circle far behind.

EVIE

Evie was starting to think she should've stuck it out with the sticky-fingered toddlers. Cars, bicyclists, skateboarders, joggers—she was surrounded by feet and wheels all determined to *go-go-go* as fast as possible. And this dog was moving faster than any of them.

He was nimble and light-footed and swift. In fact, with his pointy ears, orange-and-white fur, and sly gaze, Evie couldn't help wondering if he was actually a fox. Back when Laura's family had first adopted Evie, Laura had been obsessed with a movie about an impossibly cute hamster who made really terrible choices. The villain in that movie was a fox, and Evie had had endless nightmares about his gleaming black eyes and wicked smile.

And here she was, roaming around Manhattan with a fox just like that one. Evie was no smarter than that silly little hamster.

He's a dog, not a fox, she told herself, gasping for breath as the dog ducked around yet another corner. *He barked, didn't he? Foxes don't bark!*

At last, the fox—*dog!*—veered into a quiet alley and came to a halt, panting. Evie spotted an over-flowing dumpster and made a beeline for it.

"Where are you—" the dog began, but Evie had already squeezed herself into the blissfully dark space between the dumpster and the brick wall. Her pulse was a rapid *rat-a-tat-tat* in her ears as the dog peeked behind the dumpster.

"I didn't realize bunnies were such scavengers."

"What?" Evie managed to wheeze.

"Aren't you looking for food back there?"

"Food?" If she hadn't been so completely and totally traumatized, Evie might have laughed. "I couldn't possibly eat right now, I'm far too stressed. I need a few minutes to recover."

"Oh." The dog sounded slightly confused. She waited for him to go away, but he stayed put. "Well. While you recover, allow me to introduce myself. My name is Bartholomew Porpington the Third. But you can call me Bart."

Evie didn't know what to say to that. She eyed him distrustfully from her dark little crevasse.

Bart waited a few seconds, then added, "And you are?"

Trapped in a nightmare, Evie thought. "My name is Evie. You can call me . . . Evie."

"Nice to meet you, Evie," Bart said. He sounded friendly enough. But then again, so did the fox in that movie, right up until he tried to eat the hamster. "And congratulations on your great escape! I think you'll find street life is quite an improvement to pet life."

Once again, Evie was at a total loss for words. "Street life?" she managed to repeat.

"It's the *best*," Bart said, settling down on the ground and sniffing the bottom of the dumpster. "No leashes. No rules. You just do what you want, when you want."

Evie was aghast. "You mean you don't have a home?"

"Of course I do!" Bart said cheerfully. "This alley is my home. And so is that street, and Central Park, and—"

"But I mean, you don't have a *family*?" Evie could not imagine anything more upsetting. "People to love you and take care of you?"

Bart snorted. "I had an owner, if that's what you mean. Bitsy DuPont. And yes, she took care of me. But she also worked me to the bone."

"What kind of work?" Evie wondered, and Bart sat up a little straighter.

"You're looking at a former show dog," he informed her proudly. "Six Best in Show ribbons and an agility-course master, thank you very much!"

Evie had no idea what that meant, but she understood she was supposed to be impressed. "Um . . ."

"I know it's probably intimidating to be in the presence of a celebrity," Bart said, nosing a crusty brown banana peel stuck to the underside of the dumpster. "But don't worry. I'm the most humble dog you'll ever meet. I left the glitz and glamour of the show behind a long time ago, and I wouldn't trade this wild, free life I have now for all the Purina in Westminster."

Evie had no idea what *that* meant, either. But she did grasp one thing. This dog had left his home to live on the streets. *On. Purpose.*

Well, at least she knew for certain that he wasn't a fox. Foxes, after all, were notoriously clever, and this dog was clearly a few carrots shy of a bushel. The streets weren't *home*. Home was structure and peace and quiet and fresh raspberries and lots of love.

Home was *Laura*.

An intense pang of longing made Evie sit up

straight. Yes, she'd just had a traumatizing experi-
ence. And yes, the streets of the city were far more
terrifying than she'd ever imagined. But she'd run
away from Mrs. Vanderwaal for a reason.

"You say you know the streets well," she said to
Bart.

His ears perked up. "Very well. No one knows
'em better!"

"Do you know the way to Harlem?"

"Sure thing." Bart regarded her curiously. "Why
do you want to go there?"

"Because that's *my* home," Evie told him. "And
I have to get back. Will you . . . ?"

Pausing, Evie nibbled her lip. She had no reason
to trust this fox—no, dog, definitely a dog. But Evie
had no idea where Harlem was. What if she wandered in the wrong direction? What if she just got
farther and farther from home, from Laura, and
never *ever* found her way back?

"Will you help me?" she blurted out.

Bart was silent for a moment. He was staring at

her like she was a puzzle he had to solve. She stared right back, filled with determination.

"Yeah, I'll help you," Bart said finally. "If you'll help me with something, too."

Evie felt a twinge of foreboding. "What could I possibly help *you* with?"

"I need a collar," Bart told her. "This city is crawling with animal control workers looking for strays. I had a close call earlier today. If I had a collar, no one would think I was a stray. I'd just be another off-leash pet. You get it?"

Evie sort of got it. "I don't have a collar," she told him. "If I did, I'd give it to you, but—"

"No, no," Bart interrupted, a crafty expression sneaking onto his face. *Fox*, Evie thought in alarm. "I want you to steal one for me."

"You want me to *steal*—"

"I know just the shop," Bart said eagerly. "It's on the way to Harlem, too! Trust me, I know the place inside and out."

"Then why don't you do it?"

"Because Bitsy took me there all the time," Bart explained. "If I got caught, the owner would recognize me in a second, give her a call, and . . ." He shuddered. "There goes my freedom."

Evie's stomach flip-flopped. "But what if *I* get caught?"

"You won't! You're small and quiet, and besides, I have a plan." Bart leaped to his feet, tail wagging. "Come on, what do you say? You could be back in Harlem by tonight!"

Evie had started to say no, absolutely not, no *way*. Then she imagined being safely back at the bodega in just a few hours, snuggled up behind a bag of sugar. She took a deep, hesitant breath.

"Okay. I'm in."

8

 LAURA

The airport in Miami was, if possible, even more crowded than LaGuardia. Laura gripped her phone in her sweaty hand as she followed her parents outside to the long line of people waiting for taxis.

"Almost there!" Dad said cheerfully. "Flight wasn't so bad, was it?"

"Nope," Laura replied, and she meant it. *Apple's Amazing Adventure* had been a nice distraction, and she'd actually enjoyed watching the clouds pass outside the window. Even the food—a turkey wrap and mini chocolate chip cookies—had been pretty good.

But now her stress level was creeping up again. Her whole giant extended family was staying at the same hotel. And tonight would be the rehearsal dinner. Then tomorrow was the wedding and the reception. Laura wasn't going to get so much as a minute alone!

She felt guilty for even *wanting* alone time. After all, Laura was excited to see her family. It was just hard to be social for hours and hours on end without a break. No one ever really seemed to understand that. Except for Evie, of course.

Laura sighed. She would give anything to be in her nice, quiet bedroom with Evie right now, watching movies and munching on jalapeño popcorn.

The minute she and her parents were buckled safely into their cab seats, Laura opened Twitter on her phone. Her #bunnycation tweet had six likes, and one reply from someone Laura didn't know.

@rogerthisandthat: hey, this looks like the
#ColumbusCircleGridlock bunny!

Frowning in confusion, Laura tapped the hashtag, which had two thousand tweets and counting. As she scrolled through them, her stomach began to churn. Apparently, a dog and a bunny running through the streets had caused chaos in Columbus Circle as cars swerved to avoid hitting them. No one was hurt, but the whole circle was like a parking lot, with cars and trucks unable to move as more piled up behind them.

Laura stopped on the first video she saw, but it only showed the traffic jam from about a block away. Feeling more uneasy by the second, Laura skimmed over dozens of blurry photos and videos. *It's not Evie*, she told herself firmly. *That's impossible.* But she couldn't help remembering the view of Columbus Circle from Mrs. Vanderwaal's living room window as she swiped her screen. Then her finger froze, poised over a tweet.

@luckyloo222: Behold! The bunny and pup that started all this #ColumbusCircleGridlock mayhem! (The gf says this dog is a Shiba Inu—anyone know if that's right?)

Laura held her breath as the video played. The tinny sound of blaring horns and angry shouts came from her phone's tiny speaker, but at first, all she could see was a few cars idling on the street. Then she saw the dog.

He was orange and white, with pointy ears and a fluffy tail that curled up like a question mark. He seemed to be really agitated, barking loudly at a car in the middle lane and hopping from side to side like a boxer.

The last two seconds of the video were a blur. A tiny gray ball of fuzz darted out from under the car's front tire, the person holding the phone let out a shout, and the dog raced off, followed by the fuzzy gray ball.

Laura watched the video over and over again. The animal, whatever it was, moved too quickly for her to get a really good look. Just because it was the right size, and the right color, that didn't mean . . .

When the video started for the dozenth time, Laura finally noticed the building on the other side of the street. The entrance, with its black awning and the gold numbers *310* blazoned across the front, was familiar. Because Laura had walked through that entrance with her mom and Evie earlier that morning.

Suddenly shaking, Laura lowered her phone and turned to her parents. "Mom, we have to call Mrs. Vanderwaal *right now*."

9

 BART

Bart left Evie hunkered down behind the dumpster and ventured out of the alley. After all that running, his stomach was growling again. And despite her protestations about not being hungry, Evie had to eat *something*, right? Food always helped Bart feel better when he was stressed. Or sad. Or happy.

Really, Bart didn't need an excuse to eat.

He'd barely trotted a block when he spotted another street meat vendor. Several people waited in line as the vendor turned the skewers of meat over on the grill one by one, sending up curls of smoke.

The sizzling sound was enough to make Bart's mouth water. He crept up behind the vendor, waited until he handed a skewer to the next customer in line, then hopped up and snatched the end of one of the sticks in his teeth.

Bart took off like a shot, inhaling the irresistible smell of grilled meat. By the time he heard the vendor let out a shout, he was already veering into the alley.

He found Evie exactly where he'd left her, eyes closed as if she were meditating. Triumphantly, Bart dropped his bounty right in front of her, and her eyes flew open.

"What . . . is *that*?"

Bart tilted his head. "Street meat! It's delicious. Try it!"

He expected Evie to look excited, or at least curious. Instead, she reeled back in horror.

"Street??? *Meat*???" she repeated, horrified.

"Yeah! There's all sorts of street food in the city, but this is by far the best." As if to prove it, Bart leaned over and snatched the first cube of meat off the stick. He gobbled it down with great enthusiasm, making a show of licking his chops. Evie remained frozen in terror. Bart's tail dropped. "I thought it'd cheer you up. This is my favorite food."

Evie blinked. "Um. Well. While I appreciate this, um . . . *food*, we bunnies are herbivores. We only eat plants," she added when Bart looked confused. "You know, lettuce, berries, that sort of thing."

How utterly boring, Bart thought, but he didn't want to be rude. "I see," he said instead, glancing down at the cubes of meat. "Well, if you're sure . . ."

"Quite sure. If you're still hungry, feel free to— oh, you already did." As Bart swallowed the last cube whole, Evie stared at him with a mixture of revulsion and admiration. "How long has it been since you last ate? A day? A week?"

"An hour," Bart replied, licking the stick clean. "Hey, there's a market just down the street with lots of leafy green stuff. Want me to swipe something for you?"

"No, thank you," Evie said politely. "I'm still far too stressed to eat."

Bart sat back on his haunches. "Stressed about what?" he asked, confused.

Evie looked flabbergasted. "About . . . about *everything*!" she cried. "I'm lost in Manhattan! Laura abandoned me! I have to *steal* a *collar* for a dog I just *met* and there are so many people and bicycles and cars and loud noises and it's all just. Too. *Much*."

As she spoke, she burrowed farther back behind the dumpster. Bart felt a wave of pity for her. This poor bunny had been way too sheltered all her life—and Bart knew a little something about having an overprotective, controlling owner. Evie had practically been kept prisoner by this Laura, spending her whole life trapped inside when big, beautiful, exciting Manhattan had been waiting for her just outside the doors.

Suddenly, Bart's mission was clear. He would help Evie find her way back home to Harlem, just like he promised. But along the way, he'd show her how *amazing* street life really was. By the time they got to her convenience store, Evie might even change her mind about wanting to go home. Bart would prove to her that the free and wild life was the only way to go.

"You're right," he said, and Evie looked surprised. "The city can be pretty chaotic, and Harlem is pretty far from here. But don't worry—I know a few tricks to help get around faster. In fact..." Inspiration struck, and Bart jumped up, tail wagging fiercely. "...I just had a *great* idea! Think you can make it a few blocks back to Central Park?"

Evie hesitated. Then she visibly steeled herself. "Yes, I can. Lead the way."

"Great!" Bart trotted to the end of the alley, checking to make sure Evie was right behind him. "Now, there are so many dogs in Manhattan that, most of the time, no one gives me a second look. But it's not often you see a bunny roaming around, so I think it's best if you keep out of sight as much as possible."

"How am I going to do that?" Evie wondered, her eyes shining with fear as she peered out at the street.

"When I say go, run out and hide under there as quick as you can," Bart said, gesturing with his nose to a beat-up old sedan parked along the curb. "Ready . . . set . . . *go*!"

Evie shot across the street like a cannon, and Bart couldn't help but admire her speed. He ambled toward the sedan, glancing around casually to see if anyone had noticed the bunny. But everyone was too wrapped up in their own personal missions, eyes straight ahead or staring down at their phones. Bart stopped next to the sedan and leaned down to see Evie, pretending to lick his paw.

"Now, just follow me," he said. "But stay under the cars."

"What if one starts moving and crushes me?" Evie asked worriedly, eyeing the giant tire in front of her.

"If the car is quiet, you're safe," Bart explained. "If it's making that rumbly sound, stay away. Tell you what—stay a few steps behind me. I'll let you know if it's safe to go to the next car."

"Okay," Evie whispered. Straightening up, Bart strolled down the sidewalk, sticking close to the sedan. He kept his nose to the ground, pretending to sniff idly, but his ears were on alert.

The next car, a boxy convertible, was quiet. So was the curvy sports car after that. But the space at the end of the block was taken up by a big delivery truck, engine rumbling loudly as a skinny man in shorts and a button-down shirt carried a stack of boxes up the steps to an apartment building. Bart paused next to the sports car, pretending to examine the shiny wheel.

"Let's wait for this truck to move," he told Evie. "Another car will park, and when the driver leaves, we'll keep going."

"What if no one parks there?" Evie wondered.

"Oh, someone will," Bart replied knowingly. "Parking spots never stay open more than a few seconds around here."

He watched as the delivery guy climbed back into the truck. As the truck slowly crept back onto the street, Bart moved forward a few inches—and his rump grazed the sports car's tire.

WEEE-OOO-WEEE-OOO-WEEE-OOO!

Evie shouted something Bart couldn't hear over the alarm. The next thing he knew, the bunny flew out from under the sports car and zoomed down the sidewalk!

"Wait!" Bart cried, sprinting after her and cursing himself for not being more careful. Fancy-looking cars like that always had those obnoxious alarms that went off if so much as a leaf grazed them. He should have known better.

There were shouts and gasps as Evie zipped through a crowd of pedestrians, Bart hot on her heels. He managed to catch up to her right before the next intersection, glancing up at the taxi turning onto the street. Bart locked eyes with the driver, who scowled and slammed on the brakes.

"Keep going!" Bart nudged Evie, and the two

sped across the street and down the next block. Bart could see the thick green trees of Central Park just ahead, and he put on an extra burst of speed. At the end of the block, he ducked under a police car parked next to the curb. Evie scooted in after him, pressing up against his side. He could feel her heart practically vibrating against her ribs.

"What *was* that?"

"Car alarm," Bart explained. "It's meant to scare off thieves."

"Well, it's very effective," Evie grumbled. She peeked out from under the car. "Are we going to hide in the park?"

"No, I have a better idea," Bart said grandly. "I know a way we can travel to the north end of the park completely hidden—and in style. Madam, your carriage awaits!"

He gestured to the old-fashioned white carriage parked near the entrance to the park, spoke wheels gleaming, cover pulled over the bench seat to shade riders from the blazing sunshine. The driver, a woman in a top hat and cape, called out cheerfully to passersby, looking for her next customers. A few stopped to smile at the black horse standing in front of the carriage, admiring the giant white flowers woven around his reins.

Bart turned to Evie expectantly. He'd seen the way women swooned over the idea of a horse-and-carriage ride. It was glamorous and romantic, and he was very, very proud of himself for having thought of it.

But Evie was not swooning. On the contrary, she looked as if she was on the verge of yet another panic attack. He followed her gaze and realized she wasn't looking at the carriage but the horse.

"I know they look intimidating, but horses are very gentle!" Bart assured her. "Besides, we'll be in the carriage—see the bench with the back facing where the driver sits? There's always a blanket or two in there to cover the horse if the flies get too bad. We'll hide under that. You won't be able to see the horse, and we'll be totally invisible the whole ride!"

Evie didn't respond. She didn't move, either. Bart could practically feel the fear radiating off her. Once again, he couldn't help but pity this poor, frightened bunny who'd been raised to be afraid of the whole world.

"All we have to do is get on that carriage before the driver finds her next customers," he told her, trying to sound as confident and reassuring as possible. "Then you'll be snug under a blanket all the way to the north end of the park, at 110th Street. And that's Harlem!"

At this, Evie's ears twitched. Slowly, she tore her gaze from the horse and looked at Bart. "Really?"

"Yes!" Bart's tail thumped twice against the concrete. "The very south end of Harlem, but still. It's the best way to cover a lot of distance without being seen. Unless you want to try sneaking on the subway . . ."

Evie shuddered. "I guess the carriage is the least terrifying option."

Trying not to laugh, Bart peered out at the street

again. He could see the lights changing at the intersection, the stream of cars heading south to north slowing, the cars waiting to turn left on Central Park West edging forward.

"Now's our chance," Bart said, crouching low. "Stay close, okay? Ready . . . *go!*"

The two darted out from under the police car and into the street during the brief lull. Bart chanced a glance to his right and caught a glimpse of the statue in the middle of Columbus Circle. He could still hear the distant honks and shouts and wondered what all the ruckus was about.

He herded Evie around the carriage, to where the driver was chatting with a young man and woman.

"So where are you two visiting from?"

"Houston, Texas," the woman chirped, bouncing on her toes with excitement. "I've been here once before on a school trip. I knew ever since then that when I got married, our honeymoon would be in New York!"

"Well, congratulations!" the driver exclaimed, oblivious as Bart leaped nimbly into the carriage. He turned, staring down at Evie. But her eyes were glued to the horse.

"Come on," Bart hissed, but Evie didn't move.

"We have tickets to a Broadway show tonight," the woman rambled on. "And tomorrow we're doing a cruise on the Hudson!"

"Don't forget the Met," the man added, squeezing her hand.

"Sounds perfect!" the driver said with a big grin. "In fact, the only thing I can think of to make this honeymoon even more romantic is a horse-and-carriage ride along Central Park."

Bart leaned over as far as he dared. *"Evie. Jump."*

The bunny finally looked up at him, just as the woman let out a squeal of delight. Her husband pulled out his wallet, and Bart willed Evie to move.

After an excruciatingly long second, Evie jumped up into the carriage.

"Quick, under here." Bart scrambled under the bench, where, just as he'd predicted, a musty, hot blanket waited. Evie squirmed beneath the blanket, and Bart settled in next to her, trying to hide his relief as the couple climbed onto the carriage. It rocked slightly under their weight as they sat on the opposite bench. Bart heard the driver climb into her seat. A few moments later, the carriage jerked forward, and Evie tensed beside him.

"We did it!" Bart whispered. "It's okay, Evie. We're home free!"

Evie didn't respond. But after several minutes passed with nothing but the gentle sway of the carriage and the steady *clip-clop* of the horse's hooves, she finally started to relax.

"This is kind of nice," she admitted, giving him a small smile.

Bart felt extremely pleased with his own brilliance. For about five seconds. Then . . .

"Um, is that blanket moving?"

The woman's chirpy voice sounded more curious

than afraid, but Bart froze. Next to him, Evie held her breath.

"Probably just the wind," the man replied.

"It's not windy, silly!"

Silence followed, and Bart wished he could see what was happening. Had the couple gone back to sightseeing? Or were they still watching the blanket?

"I'm telling you, there's something under that blanket."

Before Bart had a chance to brace himself, the woman kicked gently at the blanket—and Evie leaped three feet into the air, exposing Bart!

The woman's scream was earsplitting, and her husband let out a shout of surprise. Bart caught a quick glimpse of their wide eyes and O-shaped mouths before Evie and the blanket landed. But their cover was very obviously blown.

"What's going on?" came the driver's voice, and a second later, the blanket was tugged away. The couple gaped at Bart and Evie, and Bart adopted his best puppy-dog eyes. Now that the shock had worn off, he thought maybe this would turn out okay. The woman's expression was already softening.

"Oh my goodness," she said, clasping her hands to her chest. "Are these your pets?"

"My what?" The driver peered over the seat, her eyes flying open at the sight of the furry twosome blinking up at her. *"Whoa!"*

The carriage immediately began to slow as the horse let out a loud whinny—and apparently, that was the last straw for Evie. To Bart's horror, she leaped off the still-moving carriage and into the street!

"Oh no!" cried the woman as Bart lurched forward just in time to see Evie roll *under* the carriage. Without a second thought, he tumbled after her.

The next few seconds were a terrifying jumble of dodging wheels and hooves. Bart threw himself on top of Evie just as the carriage rolled to a stop.

He pulled back and inspected her carefully as the driver and couple chattered excitedly overhead.

"You okay?" he asked urgently.

In response, Evie wrinkled her nose. Bart smelled it, too. He glanced up in time to see the horse's tail raise. And then:

SPLAT.

Neither Bart nor Evie moved. The horse's waste had landed two inches to Evie's left. It was roughly the same size and shape as Evie herself.

The carriage rocked as the driver hopped out, quickly followed by the couple.

"What happened?" the driver cried.

"There was a dog and a bunny under the seat and they jumped off the carriage!" the woman exclaimed.

"Oh no—did we run over them?"

The man's upside-down face appeared to Bart's right. He grinned, and that was upside down, too.

"They're okay!" he said.

"What should we do?" his wife asked.

"We have to go!" Bart said urgently, but Evie couldn't take her eyes off the rabbit-sized mound of poop. More feet were stopping around the carriage, more eyes peering underneath. Bart's heart was beating faster now than it had when Evie had jumped off the carriage.

"Oh my god, it's Bunny and Canine!" came a new voice.

"What?" asked the driver.

"Haven't you checked Twitter?" the first person said excitedly. "They caused that giant traffic jam in Columbus Circle!"

"Whoa, it *is* them! Should we call animal control?"

Evie still hadn't budged, and Bart was done waiting. Quickly but carefully, he picked her up with his teeth by the scruff. Then he bolted out from under the carriage, weaving around legs.

Now the driver sounded excited, too. "It's them, it's Bunny and Canine!"

"Are you getting video of this?" someone asked.

The woman squealed. "He's carrying the bunny like it's a puppy, look!"

Their voices faded as Bart raced into the park with Evie. He had no idea why these people were all so excited over the two of them, but he had a feeling no good could come of it.

10

 EVIE

Evie was totally traumatized. Again.

She bounced along helplessly, dangling from Bart's mouth. Although she could feel his strong teeth gripping her fur, his hold was surprisingly gentle. In fact, this was a much less stressful way to travel than that horrifying horse-and-carriage ride. Except for all the people surrounding them, pointing and shouting and holding up their phones as Bart and Evie raced into Central Park.

Bart darted behind the first bush he passed and carefully placed Evie on the ground. She instinctively scooted as far under the bush as she could, inhaling the comforting, leafy green scent.

"Well, that was a close call!" Bart said cheerfully. Evie stared at him in disbelief. Did *nothing* rile this dog up?

"A close call?! That woman kicked us! The carriage could have run over us! And I was nearly crushed to death by *horse poop*!"

Bart's snout twitched. "Yeah, it was pretty funny."

"*Funny?!*" Evie was outraged. "That's it. The deal is off."

"What?"

"I'm not stealing any collar, and I'm not following you anywhere."

Rather than look upset, Bart merely seemed confused. "But how will you get home?"

"I won't." Evie's voice broke, but she meant it. "I'll live here in the park. There's plenty of tall grass and bushes and places for a bunny to burrow."

"But—"

"I'm. Not. Leaving."

Bart blinked several times as Evie glared at him. Deep down, she knew she was being a little too harsh with Bart. After all, he'd only been trying to help. But Evie had experienced more trauma in the last few hours than she had in her entire life, and she was *done*.

"Okay," Bart said at last. "Well . . . good luck, Evie."

She watched him trot away, his fluffy tail dragging on the ground, and felt a strange mix of relief and regret. Bart ambled along a trail, mingling with the joggers and walkers. When he disappeared from view, Evie let out a long, slow breath.

She stayed huddled under the bush for another minute or two, enjoying the solitude. Her tummy rumbled, and she nibbled on a blade of grass. So this was her life now. A stray bunny in Central Park. It would be fine, Evie told herself, chewing harder on the grass. Sure, there were tons of people around, but it was easy enough to stay out of sight here.

Except someone *was* watching her.

Evie stopped chewing. Her fur rose slowly, and her eyes darted around. Not a single passerby seemed to noticed the small bunny beneath the bush, but some instinct Evie didn't even know she had was alerting her to the fact that she was being watched.

A slight, ruffling motion in the trees above caused her to look up—and her heart skipped a few beats. A hawk was perched on one of the lowest branches, brown-and-white feathers ruffling in the wind. And its hard yellow eyes were fixed directly on Evie.

She wasn't being watched. She was being *stalked*.

Every muscle in Evie's body clenched, and her mind screamed at her to run. But if she fled the cover of the bush and ran out in the open, the hawk would surely catch her. Evie was quick, but she couldn't outrun anything that could *fly*.

She spit out the blade of grass and tried to think. What other options did she have? She couldn't literally stay under this bush forever. But the hawk didn't look like it was going anywhere anytime soon. Evie had no doubt it would sit right there on that branch, patiently waiting for Evie to dart out. And then it would swoop down and snatch her up and—

Whimpering, Evie hunched lower to the ground. She forced herself to take her eyes off the hawk and look around. There were lots of people out, but would any of them protect her from the hawk? Evie couldn't be sure. Certainly not sure enough to take the risk.

A large group strolled by, five adults and six children. The youngest, a little boy with freckles all over his face and arms, was carrying a giant picnic basket.

"Sure you don't want help with that, Roger?" an older girl asked, smirking as the little boy stumbled under its weight.

"I can do it!" he said stubbornly, and the adults smiled at one another.

Evie stared at the basket as the boy drew closer.

Two flaps, one on either side—she could jump up and slip inside without him noticing. Maybe. But even if he did notice, Evie would rather deal with a little boy than a hawk. And, she reasoned, if the hawk *did* swoop down and try to grab the basket, the boy's family would surely protect him—and Evie.

It was still a risk. And Evie wasn't the sort of bunny who took risks. She knew what Bart would say. He'd tell her it'd be easy. He'd probably even try to convince her it'd be *fun*, trying to outrun a hungry hawk.

"Wuh-oh!" The little boy glanced down at his left shoe, which had come untied. Unnoticed by his family, he set the basket down and clumsily began to tie the laces.

This was the best chance Evie would get. Glancing up at the statue-still hawk, she took a deep breath. Then she burst out of the bushes and made a bee-line for the basket.

Evie didn't dare look up, but she heard the light

rustle of the branch as the hawk dove. *Faster, faster, faster!* About a foot from the basket, Evie leaped as far as she could. She landed on the basket, bounced off, then slipped beneath the lid in one fluid movement. A split second later, there was a *whoosh* as the hawk passed overhead, followed by a frustrated screech.

"Whoa, Mommy! Did you see that bird!" the little boy cried. Evie stayed perfectly still, trying to hear over the rapid *pat-pat-pat* of her heartbeat.

"What bird?" came a woman's voice. "Roger, what are you doing?"

"Tying my shoe!" the boy replied proudly.

"Do you need help with the basket?"

"No." There was a lurch, a little grunt, and a *thud* as the boy set the basket down hard. "Yes."

Evie tensed as footsteps approached. A moment later, Roger's mom lifted the basket, and Evie bumped against a baguette.

"Oof, this is pretty heavy," the woman said. "You did a great job carrying it all this way, little man!"

The basket swayed slightly as she walked, and Roger began to chatter excitedly about the giant bird that had flown right over his head. With every second that passed, Evie relaxed a tiny bit more. She'd done it. She'd outrun a *hawk*. The relief made her feel almost giddy.

See? she imagined Bart saying. *Told you it'd be fun!*

It was NOT fun, Evie argued in her head. *It was dangerous!* But in the darkness of the basket, she smiled to herself.

After a few minutes, Evie felt brave enough to nudge the lid up just a little bit and peer outside. The path must have veered deeper into Central Park, because Evie couldn't hear the sounds of traffic anymore. A massive green lawn spread out to her left, framed by thick, bushy trees and, farther back, towering skyscrapers set against a bright blue sky.

Wow, Evie thought, momentarily forgetting her predicament. *The city really is beautiful.*

Then she shook herself. Beautiful things could

still be dangerous. She was about to duck back into the basket when something caught her eye.

It was Bart! Evie raised the lid a little bit higher. The dog was much farther ahead on the path, but his floofy tail and swishy, confident trot were unmistakable. Evie half wanted to chase after him and tell him all about her close encounter with the hawk. Then something else—no, some*one* else—caught her eye.

A young, skinny man was hiding behind a tree. He wasn't hiding from the people passing by, but his posture was a little too still, like he didn't want to be spotted. But the most alarming thing was the stick in his hand, with a steel loop at the end. Evie didn't know what it was for, but she didn't like the looks of it. She followed the man's gaze and felt her stomach plummet.

He was watching Bart.

No, not watching. *Stalking.* Just like the hawk had stalked Evie. As Bart rounded a curve and dis-appeared from sight, the young man slipped out from behind the tree, holding the stick with the loop high, and followed.

Without giving herself a chance to think about it, Evie leaped from the picnic basket and raced after them.

11

 LAURA

Laura stared out the front window of the taxi, where brakes flashed bright red like emergency lights. She curled her fingers into fists and listened as her mom spoke to Mrs. Vanderwaal.

"Oh my goodness. Okay . . . Oh, Wentworth, too? I'm so . . . Oh, please, Blair, don't apologize. I know you would never . . . What's that? Yes, yes of course. I'll give you a call once we're at the hotel."

Exhaling slowly, Mom hung up and set her phone in her lap.

"What's going on?" Dad asked, but Laura already knew. She'd known even before she'd heard Mrs. Vanderwaal's tinny, strained voice on the other end of the phone.

Mom kept her voice calm. "Evie got out of the apartment. Blair's sister is visiting with her niece and nephew, and they left the front door open for just a minute. She feels absolutely terrible. But they're looking for Evie, honey," she added, turning to Laura. "And she's calling for volunteers at the shelter to help. They'll find her!"

Finally, Laura tore her eyes from the traffic scene out the window and turned to face her parents. Their faces were filled with worry, although she knew it was more worry for her than for Evie. Laura said nothing; she just nodded mutely.

"And did I hear her say her cat got out, too?" Dad asked.

"Yes, although apparently Wentworth sneaks out all the time," Mom said quickly. "But he always comes back. Maybe they're together!"

"They're not." Feeling light-headed, Laura picked up her phone. "I don't know where Wentworth is, but Evie and a dog caused a giant traffic jam in Columbus Circle."

"What?" Mom and Dad said at the same time. Laura opened Twitter and found the video of Evie and the dog racing across the street.

"We can't be sure that's Evie," Dad said, his brow furrowing as the video played a second time. "It might not even be a bunny. It could be a cat, or—"

"No, Jorge, look," Mom interrupted, blinking in disbelief. "That's Mrs. Vanderwaal's building."

"It's definitely Evie." Laura's voice came out flat. She always thought that in a real emergency, she'd be in a complete panic: wobbly voice, uncontrollable sobbing, all of that. But she felt weirdly calm. Worried, yes. *Very* worried. But she spent so much time feeling anxious that the worst *might* happen, that once it actually happened, her nerves just vanished. Or maybe this was some next-level anxiety, and her body was going into a numb sort of autopilot.

She scrolled through the gridlock hashtag, stopping when a different video popped up. Holding her breath, Laura skimmed the tweet quickly.

@MTSchneiderman: #ColumbusCircleBunny and friend crashed a newlywed couple's horse and carriage ride!!! Look at these two outlaws go! 😂 #BunnyandCanine

Laura's parents leaned over to watch the video. The person holding the phone was strolling down Central Park West just as a horse and carriage passed by. Suddenly, there was a scream and a shout of "Whoa!" The next part happened fast: a flurry of movement as two squirming balls of fur fell from the carriage, one right after the other, at the same time as the horse came to a halt. The driver stood to look back at the carriage, where a young couple was already scrambling to get out. A crowd had just started to gather, everyone stooping over to see beneath the carriage—and then the orange-and-white Shiba Inu burst out, dodging around legs and passing right by the person holding the phone. And in his mouth . . . was *Evie*.

Panic bolted through Laura as she watched the dog race into the park before the video ended. "Is he going to eat Evie?" Whatever calm she'd felt before was gone, and the words came out almost like a shriek.

Mom placed her hand firmly on Laura's back. "Breathe, honey," she said, and Laura drew in a ragged breath. The video was playing again, and when the dog darted past the phone, Mom tapped the screen to pause it. "Look, he's holding her just like she's a puppy! I don't think he's trying to eat her. In fact, it looks like he's *rescuing* her."

Hot tears filled Laura's eyes. "Really? Are you just saying that to make feel better?"

"No, your mother's right," Dad said, nodding. "It looks like Evie fell out of the carriage, and the dog jumped after her. Then he carried her to safety!"

Laura looked from Mom to Dad, then back at

the screen. She watched the video for a third time, and now she could see what they meant. The Shibu Inu wasn't trying to hurt Evie. He might have even saved her from being trampled by a horse!

The knot in her stomach loosened but only a little bit. Now Laura's poor bunny was lost in Central Park. She was getting farther and farther from Mrs. Vanderwaal's apartment by the second. And Laura was across the country, unable to help look for her.

Wait—that wasn't true! Struck with inspiration, Laura glanced at the new hashtag one more time, then sent another tweet of her own.

> @JALBodegaBunny: HELP! My name is Evie and I'm lost in
> Central Park. Last spotted with a (friendly!) orange and
> white dog. Please reply to this account if you spot me!
> #BunnyandCanine #ColumbusCircleGridlock

Mom read over her shoulder and chuckled. "Bunny and Canine, that's cute."

"What's it mean?" Laura asked as she sent the tweet.

"I'm pretty sure it's a pun on Bonnie and Clyde," Mom explained. "They were two outlaws back in the 1930s who traveled across the country, robbing banks and stores and evading the police at every turn."

Laura wished she could laugh at the idea of a bunny and a dog as fugitives running from the law. But she couldn't stop picturing Evie dangling helplessly from the dog's mouth. How far into the park would he take her? And then where would they go? Evie loved small, cozy spaces and familiar toys, and now she was in the great, open expanse of Central Park. *She must be so scared*, Laura thought, her throat tightening.

The taxi exited the highway, picking up speed as they left the traffic behind.

"Hey, I think I see our hotel," Dad said, trying to sound cheerful.

Mom's hand was still on Laura's back. "Mrs. Vanderwaal will keep in touch," she whispered. "Try to relax, okay, hon? Hey, I bet your cousins are going to be thrilled to see you!"

Laura nodded, not trusting herself to speak. As the taxi pulled into the hotel's circular driveway, she closed her eyes. How was Laura going to get through this whole weekend when her best friend was lost in Manhattan?

12

 BART

With every step Bart took, the urge to turn around and go back to find Evie grew stronger. After all, she'd been the best chance he had at finally getting a collar. Bart's plan had been pretty much fool-proof. But without Evie, there was no way he could pull it off.

And maybe that wasn't the only reason he wanted to go back. Bart didn't want to admit it—Evie had sort of hurt his feelings, after all he'd done to help her—but he was worried about her. Evie was still so delusional that she actually *wanted* to return to a life as that Laura girl's prisoner.

Besides, in the half hour that Bart had known Evie, she'd nearly been run over by a car and a horse and carriage. The truth was, that sheltered little bunny had no idea how to survive in the wilds of Manhattan. Whether she wanted Bart around or not, she couldn't survive without him.

Bart slowed his pace as the reservoir came into view. Hurt feelings or no, he really should go back and make sure Evie was okay. It was the right thing to do.

With a decisive nod, Bart turned around—and a steel loop slipped around his neck.

"Gotcha, little guy!"

Stunned, Bart found himself staring up into the face of Jeff the dogcatcher. Up close, he was even younger than Bart had thought, with a smatter of acne around his nose and a wide smile that would've looked friendly if Bart hadn't known any better.

Jeff tugged on the pole that was connected to the loop, and Bart had a sudden flash of what would happen next: the truck, the animal shelter, the dreaded cage . . .

No more freedom.

Panic surged through Bart, and he pulled hard against the loop. But it was no use. Jeff was surprisingly strong for such a skinny guy, and Bart found himself lurching forward despite his efforts to plant his paws in the ground. *This was it,* he thought dismally. *This was the end.*

Suddenly, Jeff let out a yelp, and the pressure around Bart's neck loosened as the dogcatcher lost his grip on the pole. "Get off! What the—"

Jeff hopped on one foot, swatting at something small and gray that was leaping around his legs. Bart blinked several times, unable to believe his eyes.

"Evie?!"

Jeff let out a little howl as Evie nipped one of his bare ankles, then dropped the pole. Evie leaped onto Bart's back, her tiny paws digging into his fur.

"Run!" Evie cried.

Bart didn't hesitate. He took off for the reservoir

as fast as he could manage with a bunny on his back and a steel pole dragging alongside him. Jeff sprinted after them, shouting for help, as people started to stare—and take out their phones.

Putting on an extra burst of speed, Bart turned onto the path that curved around the giant reservoir. The steel pole was making a loud scraping noise against the concrete, and between the loop around his neck and the weight of Evie on his back, Bart knew he couldn't run much longer. Then he spotted a tree up ahead, and just like that, he had a plan.

"Hide behind that tree," he managed to gasp, slowing his pace just a little. "Wait till I give you the signal!"

"And then what?" Evie asked.

Bart grinned. "You'll know what to do!"

Evie hopped off and scampered over to the tree. Bart veered left, heading straight for the railing that ran between the path and the water. Jeff's shouts grew closer, and Bart's pulse quickened as he squeezed into the gap between the railing and the ground. For one heart-stopping moment, the loop caught on one of the rails, trapping him—but with a little wiggling, Bart managed to pull free just in time.

"Stop right there!" came a voice from behind them.

Jeff arrived, out of breath and red in the face, staring down at Bart over the railing. Bart stood precariously balanced on the little bit of concrete path that stuck out on the other side of the railing. Behind him was about a foot's drop into the water.

Jeff held up his hands as if in surrender. "Okay, little guy. Nice try, but you're stuck now. Let me help you, okay? Just stay right there . . ."

As he spoke, he stretched his long, lanky body over the railing and reached down. Bart forced himself to remain still as the dogcatcher's hand grazed his fur. He glanced at the tree and saw Evie peeking out from behind the trunk, watching. When Jeff's fingers closed around the pole and he lifted it up,

Bart drew a sharp breath and let out a single, sharp bark.

"Now!"

As Evie darted out from behind the tree, Bart slipped easily from the loop. Jeff let out a cry of surprise. He swiped at Bart with his free hand, but Bart dodged out of the way and slipped back underneath the railing just as Evie leaped into the air—

—and bit Jeff right on the butt!

"YAHHH!" Jeff yelled, lurching forward. An instant later, there was a loud *SPLASH*!

"Oh my gosh, someone help him!"

"He was trying to save that dog!"

"I think that bunny bit him!"

Bart and Evie whirled around as dozens of people raced toward them from all directions. Behind him, Bart could hear Jeff sputtering and shouting from the water. He glanced at Evie and was shocked to see she didn't looked frightened.

In fact, she almost looked like she was enjoying herself.

"Time to run again?" she said, and Bart grinned. "Let's go!"

They raced joyfully down the path together, leaving the dogcatcher and a crowd of people snapping pictures and taking videos behind them.

"This is the best market in Manhattan," Bart told Evie. The two of them had walked through the park for hours before venturing back into the city. "It's on a pretty quiet street, and the owner won't mind us hiding out for a while. He *loves* dogs."

Evie's ears flattened against her head. "What about bunnies?"

"I can't imagine he'd have any problem with bunnies," Bart said reassuringly.

But the truth was, he had no idea. Bart hadn't lied to Evie, exactly. The owner, a round man with a shiny bald head named Marcus, always greeted him jovially. And he always, *always* had something delicious for Bart to eat.

It was the part about the owner not minding

them hiding out that was maybe sort of not entirely true. Bart slept at the market a lot; the owner just didn't know about it. But Bart didn't see any reason to tell Evie that.

Besides, she *had* to be hungry by now, right? After all that running, Bart was absolutely starving.

"There it is!" he said triumphantly, breaking into a trot when he spotted the familiar yellow-and-orange awning. Evie scurried after him as he led the way around the side.

Marcus was unpacking a crate of oranges, piling them up high next to the display of kiwis. His face lit up when he saw Bart.

"Well, hey there!" he called in his booming voice, and Bart's tail wagged furiously. "How's my favorite little guy? Oh, hey now." Marcus's eyes widened when he spotted Evie. "Got yourself a girlfriend, do you?"

Crouching down, he held his hand out for Evie to sniff. The bunny froze on the sidewalk, staring at his fingers in horror. After a moment, Marcus chuckled.

"Skittish thing, aren't ya?" He winked at Bart. "Come on back, little guy. I've got a surprise for you—and I'm sure I can scare up something for your friend, too."

A few minutes later, Bart was digging into leftover slices of juicy steak, cooked rare, just the way he liked it. Marcus had set out a paper plate piled with kale and plump, juicy blueberries for Evie, but she had yet to take a bite.

Bart finished his steak in record time and licked his chops, then licked the plate for good measure. "Aren't you going to eat?" he asked finally.

Evie quivered. "I'm not hungry."

Her tummy rumbled loudly as if on cue, and Bart snorted. Even Evie cracked a smile.

"Well, maybe I could eat a *little*."

She took the tiniest blueberry on the plate and ate it slowly and methodically. Then she ate another . . . and another . . . and another. Bart watched, amused, as the bunny polished off every single berry before moving on to the pile of kale.

"This is *really* good," Evie said, gnawing on a stem.

"Told you!" Bart settled into a more comfortable position. "Marcus is the best."

"He does seem very nice," Evie admitted. "I bet he'd make a great owner."

Bart cocked his head. "He is the owner. I told you that."

"No, I mean a pet owner," Evie said.

Something about the way she said it was a bit too casual. Bart narrowed his eyes.

"I don't *want* an owner."

"I didn't say you did!" Evie selected another kale leaf without looking at him. "I just said he'd make a good owner. Like Laura and her parents."

"If Laura's so great, why'd you run off?"

"I didn't run away from *her*!" Evie said defensively. "I ran away from Mrs. Vanderwaal."

"Who's Mrs. Vanderwaal?"

"Some lady. Laura and her mom brought me to her apartment this morning."

"Why?"

"Because . . ." Evie swallowed. "I don't know, to be honest."

The two of them fell silent. Bart felt terribly bad for Evie. Why couldn't she see how much better off she was without an owner?

"Bitsy fed me steak sometimes," he said, and Evie looked up. "Always the best food. She had me groomed once a week. She bought me the most expensive toys and bed and everything."

Evie watched him closely. "Then why did you run away?"

"Because that stuff doesn't make someone a good owner." Bart glanced at the market's entrance. He couldn't see Marcus, but he could hear him whistling. "It doesn't mean someone actually cares about you. It doesn't mean they actually lo—"

He stopped, then shook his head. "You know what? Never mind."

"Bart—"

"I'm tired," Bart said abruptly, standing and

stretching. "I'm going to crash for a while. Think you can find a place to burrow in here?"

Evie nodded. "Sure," she said quietly.

"Okay." Bart headed down the aisle without looking back. There was an empty crate tucked away under the gourmet cheese display. Marcus never seemed to notice him there—or if he did, he pretended not to.

Bart climbed inside and curled up into a ball. For a moment, he felt a ping of guilt for abandoning Evie, even though he knew she could hide— probably better than him.

Still, for some reason, Bart regretted leaving her. It was nice to have some company, for a change. But it wasn't like this was going to last. Evie was determined to go home to her owner.

And Bart was just as determined never to have an owner again.

13

 EVIE

Evie woke up the next morning and blinked, disoriented. The sunshine was so bright— Had Laura left the blinds open? And why did Laura smell so bad?

Then she remembered following Bart to the market. Meeting the very kind Marcus and enjoying a delicious meal of kale and blueberries. Snuggling up behind a massive bag of whole-grain brown rice and falling asleep. It almost felt like home.

Almost, but not quite.

A loud snore right next to her made Evie startle.

She stared at Bart, curled up into a tight little ball, his nose twitching as if he was tracking something in his sleep. After a moment, Evie relaxed and lowered her head to her paws. She must have slept *really* hard if she hadn't even noticed Bart crawling behind the bag to join her. Evie had a sudden vision of Bart at the bodega, snoring loudly in aisle three, and she almost laughed.

Every time Evie thought about the bodega and Laura, her heart twisted painfully. She was still determined to get home, even though she wasn't sure what would happen once she got there. What if the Rodriguezes were angry that Evie had run away from Mrs. Vanderwaal? Worse, what if Laura didn't want her anymore? What if Wentworth was right, and Laura had intended for Evie to live with Mrs. Vanderwaal until she found a new home?

Evie couldn't bear the thought. When Bart let out another loud snore, she smiled to herself. At least she had a friend now. And although she'd never admit it to Bart, yesterday hadn't been all bad.

Totally traumatizing, for sure. But maybe also just a tiny bit fun.

"Heel!" Bart yelped suddenly, startling himself awake. Evie jumped, eyeing him suspiciously.

"What?"

Bart stared at her, his eyes still coming into focus. "Huh?"

"You said *heel.*"

"Oh." Bart gave his head a little shake. "I was dreaming about my days in the show again." He shuddered in an exaggerated way, then bounded to his feet. "We'd better get going!"

Evie stood as well. "Are we close to the shop?"

"The shop?" Bart repeated, clearly confused.

"The shop that has the collar I'm going to steal for you."

Bart's mouth opened, then closed. "Oh, um . . . don't worry about that."

"What? Why?" Evie felt slightly panicked. "Are you not going to help me find the bodega anymore?"

"Oh, I am!" Bart reassured her. "Just . . . never mind about the collar. It's not a big deal. I don't need one."

Evie studied him. After their encounter with the dogcatcher, it was very clear to Evie that Bart *did* need a collar. Why was he suddenly pretending he didn't need her to sneak into the pet store and steal one?

Because he doesn't think I can do it, Evie realized. She couldn't blame him. But Evie had outrun a hawk! She'd bitten the dogcatcher right on the butt!

"Bart, I—"

Evie fell suddenly silent at the sound of keys rattling just outside the entrance. Bart got to his feet, his ears pricked up.

"So here's the thing," he said quickly. "Marcus doesn't exactly *let* me sleep here. He just . . . never catches me."

He cast Evie a sidelong look, clearly waiting for her to panic. But to his surprise—and to her surprise, too—Evie smiled.

"Time to run again?"

Bart grinned.

"Let's go."

Central Park was even busier than it had been yesterday. Evie stuck to Bart's side as they made their way north, keeping just off the trail and as out of sight as possible. The sun was bright, the birds were chirping, and somehow, the park seemed much less menacing than it had yesterday.

A small part of Evie even *liked* it here. She wondered what Laura would think if she could see Evie now, then banished that thought as quickly as it had come. No sense thinking about Laura now. She had to focus on getting back home to the bodega.

"What is that thing those people keep throwing at each other?" she asked Bart, nodding to the lawn on the other side of the path.

"Oh, that's a Frisbee!" Bart said enthusiastically. "I've played lots of times. Gotta be careful, though. Not everyone wants a dog to jump in on their . . ."

He trailed off, and after a moment, Evie realized he'd stopped walking. "Bart?"

Bart didn't respond. His eyes were locked on something up ahead. His tail, which had been high and swaying, now hung so low it grazed the grass.

"What is it?" Evie asked nervously, remembering the hawk. She stared around nervously, but no one— and nothing—seemed to be watching them.

"Nothing, I, uh . . ." Bart blinked. "I gotta go."

"Go?" Evie asked in alarm. "Go where?"

"No, *go*," Bart said urgently. "You know . . ." He lifted his leg slightly, and Evie let out a sigh of relief.

"Oh! Sure. I'll just wait under this bush."

But Bart was already sprinting away toward the nearest tree. Evie scooted under the cover of the bush, watching as Bart disappeared on the other side of the tree. Why had he looked so panicked? It was so unlike him.

"Heel."

Evie glanced up at the sharp voice. A tall woman

with beady eyes and gray hair pulled back in a tight bun was glowering down at a fluffy white dog. After a moment, the dog sat nervously, and the woman sighed.

"Far too slow. Let's try it again."

She started to walk, jerking the dog's leash. The dog trotted at her side, his eyes never leaving her face. Evie studied them as they passed. The woman wore a pale pink suit with matching high heels, and diamonds glittered around her neck. Her dog also wore a sparkly collar, along with a pink harness that matched the woman's suit perfectly.

"*Heel.*"

The woman stopped walking abruptly, and the dog instantly stopped at her side. After a moment, she nodded.

"Better," she said, and they continued down the path.

Evie watched them go. She couldn't help feeling sorry for the dog. Maybe Bart was right. Not all owners were like Laura.

Something sparkly caught Evie's eye on the path. Hesitantly, she looked around, then crept forward. Was that what she thought it was?

When she was sure no one was looking, Evie darted out into the path, snatched up the sparkly thing, then scurried back beneath her bush. She set her prize down and stared at it, her heart thumping a mile a minute.

The woman's diamond collar! It must have slipped off, and she'd been too focused on her dog to notice. Up close, it was extremely beautiful: a fine strand of diamonds with a big ruby pendant.

Suddenly, Evie was struck with an idea. A wonderful, amazing, *brilliant* idea.

"Evie?"

Evie's head jerked up, and she quickly positioned herself in front of the collar. "Over here!"

She watched as Bart ambled over, his tail high and swaying again.

"What are you doing on this side of the path?" Bart asked.

Evie squirmed with excitement. "Well, I . . . I found something. For you."

"What is it?"

"Your very own"—Evie hopped to the side—"collar!"

She gazed at him eagerly, so proud of herself that she thought she might burst. But something was wrong. Bart didn't look pleased. In fact, he looked sort of horrified.

"Did you steal it from—from that woman?"

"What? No!" Evie exclaimed. "It fell off her. I didn't even notice it until she was gone."

"We've got to get out of here," Bart said abruptly. "Follow me!"

He raced off without a second glance at the collar. Trying not to feel hurt, Evie picked the delicate chain of diamonds up again and hurried after him. She followed Bart out of the park and down a set of stairs.

He was taking her *underground*.

Evie's heart was racing now for a different reason.

A long, wide corridor stretched out in front of her. Not far away, she spotted a few people carrying yellow cards toward a weird door made of metal bars. One at a time, they swiped their cards on something Evie couldn't see, and when the door beeped, they pushed through and headed down even more stairs.

Evie had never seen this place before. But the sounds and smells were strangely familiar.

"Whadisdisplays?" Evie asked around the collar.

Turning, Bart let out a growl. "Why did you bring that?"

Evie was completely bewildered. "Because it's a *collar*! You need one!"

"But that's—never mind, just ditch it!" Bart ordered.

Hurt and confused, Evie hurried over to a trash can and gently placed the beautiful collar behind it.

"Come on!" Bart said, racing toward the metal door. Evie followed, and the two of them easily slipped below the bars and headed down the stairs. At the bottom, Evie froze.

A platform crowded with people spread out in front of her, and on either side was a dark tunnel. The smells were overpowering, and there was a low rumble that Evie didn't like one bit. It sounded as if a beast was lurking in one of those tunnels.

"What is this place?" she said again. Although she was pretty sure she knew.

"It's a subway station," Bart said, already heading down the platform. "We're taking the train to Harlem."

14

 LAURA

As soon as they checked in to the hotel, Laura and her parents changed into dressy clothes for the rehearsal dinner, which was at a super-fancy restaurant in the hotel. Laura was so distracted about Evie, she barely even felt nervous as she walked into the restaurant. She hung back as Dad called, "Luisa!" and hurried forward to hug his sister. Her thoughts were with Evie as Aunt Luisa introduced them to her fiancé, Roger, and even though Mom kept nudging Laura, she couldn't muster more than a smile and a mumbled, "Nice to meet you."

"Omigod, Laura!"

Laura's eyes widened, and she turned around. A moment later, Izzy, Grace, and Bianca had surrounded her. Laura felt trapped in a tornado of giggles and body lotion.

"Hi," she squeaked, allowing her cousins to drag her over to a table.

The whole evening felt like a nightmare. Laura sat there like a zombie as her cousins chattered away, seemingly oblivious to the fact that Laura wasn't responding. Then the speeches started, but Laura hardly heard a word—not even when Dad gave a toast that was apparently hilarious, judging from all the howls of laughter.

All she could think about was Evie.

The one bright spot was that since Laura wasn't at a table with her parents, they couldn't chide her for checking Twitter. Laura kept her phone on her lap, constantly refreshing her feed and searching for new #BunnyandCanine videos.

"Laura's watching doggy videos!"

Startled, Laura glanced up. Grace, her youngest cousin, was giving her a teasing look.

"Sorry," Laura said, blushing hotly. She tried to turn her phone over in her lap, but it was too late.

"Lemme see!" Izzy took the phone and stretched her arm out so her sisters could see the screen. The video of the dog and Evie scurrying out from under the carriage and running into Central Park was playing on a loop. "Aw, is that a bunny?"

"It's . . . it's *my* bunny," Laura said.

Izzy looked aghast. "You mean Evie?"

Laura nodded. Her eyes felt hot, and she struggled not to cry.

"Why's she running around with a dog?" Grace asked.

And Laura told them the whole story.

Once she started talking, she couldn't stop. The words just kept spilling out. It was probably the most she'd ever talked in front of her cousins in her whole life.

"Now she's lost in Manhattan and I'm stuck here

and I can't even look for her," Laura finished, wiping away a tear. She was so worried, she couldn't even feel embarrassed about crying in front of her cousins.

"I'm *so* sorry, Laura," said Bianca, tucking a lock of straight dark hair behind her ear. A high school freshman, she was the oldest of the cousins. "But you'll be back home tomorrow night, right? I'm sure you'll find her!"

Laura nodded and tried to smile.

Next to her, Izzy let out a squeal. "Look, there's a new video!"

She held out Laura's phone, and everyone leaned forward.

Laura couldn't believe her eyes. Someone had captured video of the Shiba Inu sprinting through Central Park with a dogcatcher's loop around his neck—*and Evie on his back!*

"It's like he's her horse!" Izzy cried, giggling uncontrollably. To be fair, Izzy laughed at almost anything, including the waiter when he'd informed her that the fish soup they were having for the first course was called *bouillabaisse*. Or, as Izzy kept calling it, "booya base!"

Laura watched the video over and over, her mind reeling. What in the world was Evie doing with that dog?

BEEP! BEEP! BEEP!

With a gasp, Laura sat up straight in an unfamiliar bed. Was that a fire alarm? A smoke detector? Blinking, she stared at the clock flashing 7:00 a.m. on her night table. *Oh*, she thought, rubbing her eyes. *Right.*

Miami. The wedding. Her cousins. Yawning, Laura turned the alarm off.

Her eyelids felt like sandpaper, scratching her eyes every time she'd blinked. Laura frowned. She'd lain awake until three in the morning, stressed about . . . about what? Then, with a rush of dread, Laura remembered.

Evie.

Now fully awake, Laura snatched her phone off the night table and unplugged the charger. She'd stayed up all night on her phone, refreshing the hashtag, but there hadn't been any new Bunny and Canine sightings.

Now Laura opened Twitter again. For a moment, she didn't understand what she was looking at. Had she accidentally swapped phones with one of her cousins? But no, this was her phone, and this was her @JALBodegaBunny account—which now had over *two thousand followers.*

Laura's mouth opened and closed. There were 353 new notifications, and she tapped to view them with a mixture of excitement and dread. The top notification was from @heymattiedee, and her message just said *Oh @JALBodegaBunny, you naughty thing!* But it was the headline of the article she'd linked that made Laura stop breathing completely.

Runaway Bunny Steals Diamond Necklace!

Numbly, Laura opened the link and a video began to play. Laura recognized Central Park West.

For a few seconds, nothing happened. Then the Shiba Inu burst out of the park and flew down the stairs into the subway. And right on his heels was Evie. Except . . .

Laura clapped her hand over her mouth. Evie had a *diamond necklace* in her mouth!

The video ended, and Laura sat staring at her phone, dumbfounded. No wonder Evie's Twitter account had gotten so many followers overnight— she really was an outlaw now!

Saturday had to be the longest day of Laura's entire life. Aunt Luisa had hired hair stylists and makeup artists for everyone, not just her and the brides-maids, so Laura had been forced to sit in a chair for almost two hours while one woman rolled her hair up in curlers and another one applied con-cealer and mascara and all kinds of stuff to Laura's face.

Her cousins were having a blast, although it took the makeup artist three tries to apply Grace's lipliner because she couldn't stop talking about her new shoes, her sisters' hair, Aunt Luisa's gown, and everything else that popped into her head.

When they were all finished, Laura stood in front of a floor-length mirror and blinked. Her dark brown curls were piled into a loose bun, held in place with several barrettes the same shade of purple as her dress. Thick strokes of black eyeliner and deep pink and brown eyeshadow made her eyes look really dramatic.

"We look uh-*mazing*!" Izzy squealed, throwing her arm around Laura and almost knocking her over in the process. Grace hurried over and linked elbows with Laura, beaming at their reflections.

"Laura, that dress is so perfect! Where'd you get it? I ordered mine online. Or, I mean, Mom did. It's from this little shop we found when we to LA last summer and . . ."

Grace continued her ramble all the way to the elevator, which the four girls squeezed onto with three bridesmaids and Laura's uncle Hector, who was apparently allergic to the bridesmaids' bouquets because he sneezed the whole ride down to the lobby. Laura tried to smile and nod along with whatever her cousins were talking about, but her mind was with Evie.

The wedding was held in one of the prettiest churches Laura had ever seen, with colorful stained glass windows and a dizzingly high arched ceiling. The ceremony was beautiful, too, but Laura had a hard time paying attention. Once, she pulled her phone out of her purse and tried to check Twitter, but then Mom gave her the stink eye and she hastily put it away again. Laura didn't want to be rude, but her bunny was on the run from the law! How was she supposed to focus?

At last, the ceremony ended, and everyone hurried outside with tiny bags of birdseed, which they threw at a beaming Aunt Luisa and Roger—now *Uncle* Roger, Laura reminded herself—as they ran down the steps toward the white limo waiting along the curb.

"I'm starving!" Grace announced dramatically, appearing at Laura's side. Bianca was there, too, adjusting a stray curl that had come loose from Grace's bun. Izzy trailed behind Bianca, eyes glued to her phone.

"There's gonna be tons of food at the reception," Bianca told her youngest sister, grinning. "And a DJ, and— Hey, Laura, you okay?"

Laura realized her eyes had filled with tears, and she blinked them back. The thought of enduring hours and hours of a big party while she was worried sick about Evie was too much.

"I'm fine," she said, but her voice cracked a little.

Grace looked heartbroken. "Laura, aren't you having fun with us?"

"Yes!" Laura replied, maybe a little too quickly. "I'm just, well . . ." After a moment, she decided simply to be honest. "I'm so worried about Evie. I guess I'm not really in a party mood."

To her surprise, Bianca smiled.

"Actually, we think we can help."

Laura stared. "How?" For a moment, she was terrified her cousins were about to suggest another dance routine.

"You can't look for Evie in Manhattan—but you *can* look for her online!" Bianca replied, waving her phone for emphasis. "*Tons* of people have taken video and photos of her. We stayed up last night tweeting at them and asking questions. We're trying to figure out where Evie and that dog might be going next!"

"We decided to be detectives!" Grace said, beaming. "And Bianca didn't even tell you the best part. We found—"

"Hey, we agreed I'd tell her this part!" Izzy cried. "*I* found him."

"Found who?" Laura asked.

"The dog!" Izzy and Grace cried at the same time.

"*What?*"

"I was looking through that hashtag, and

someone mentioned going to something called . . . Westminster?"

"Yeah, that's a really famous dog show," Laura said. She was getting more confused by the minute. "It's at Madison Square Garden every year."

"Well, this guy said the dog's breed is a"—Izzy squinted at her screen—"Shiba . . . Inu? And he thinks the dog with Evie looks a lot like the dog who got second place last year, and he linked to a YouTube video, and, well, check it out."

She held up her phone, and Laura saw a pinched-faced woman with her graying hair in a severe bun leading a Shiba Inu through the agility course. The dog moved gracefully, but the woman never smiled once, just watched him with a sour expression. As the dog leaped through another hoop, the camera zoomed in for a few seconds.

Laura bit her lip. It did look a *lot* like the dog with Evie. And he had moved so nimbly, tumbling off the carriage to save Evie, tearing through the park with Evie on his back . . .

"Oh, and the best part?" Izzy's eyes sparkled. "His name is Bartholomew Porpington the Third."

Grace burst into giggles, and Bianca rolled her eyes.

"The thing is, it doesn't make sense that a show dog would be running around the city. So maybe that's not him."

"Girls, let's go!" The four of them turned to see Uncle Hector and Aunt Ana with Laura's parents.

"Coming!" Bianca called before turning back to Laura. "But the point is, we've got a lead! And we're going to do whatever we can to help you find Evie."

"We'll keep searching," Izzy added. "Mission Bodega Bunny!"

Laura's throat tightened, only now she wanted to cry for a different reason. "You guys would really spend the whole reception helping me?"

Bianca looked surprised. "Of course we would!"

"We'll spend this whole trip searching if we have to," Izzy said, nodding vigorously.

"And eating," Grace added, rubbing her belly. "But don't worry. I can eat and search at the same time."

Laura was touched. "Thanks so much, you guys," she said. "And you know what, Grace? You just gave me a great idea."

15

 BART

Bart loved subway stations. There was always a chunk of pizza crust or some sort of treat lying around, and people down here were so focused on getting to wherever they were going that they didn't pay much attention to a stray dog wandering around.

But right now, he couldn't feel happy or excited. He couldn't believe Evie had stolen that necklace. No, not stolen, he reminded himself—she'd found it on the path. And she had no idea who that woman was who lost it.

But Bart did.

Evie stuck close to his side as he hurried down the platform. He could tell she was confused, but he didn't want to waste time with explanations right now. All Bart wanted was to get out of the Upper West Side as quickly as possible. The best way to do that was the train. The problem? Dogs weren't allowed to just walk on the train, not even on a leash. Their owners carried them in crates or, if you were a teacup Chihuahua or maybe a shih tzu, in a purse.

But that was okay. Bart had a plan.

He spotted a booth selling snacks and newspapers ahead and put on a burst of speed. Behind the register, the worker was ringing up a man's bottle of soda. In front of the booth were a few racks with magazines, paperback books, and tote bags.

"Yes," Bart said under his breath. He slowed his pace, keeping an eye on the worker as he and Evie drew closer. As the man walked away with his soda, the worker turned his attention to his phone—and Bart snatched a tote bag with a big apple on the front and took off.

"Wait, Bart!" Evie called, racing after him. But Bart didn't stop until he'd reached the end of the platform, which had fewer people. He dropped the tote bag, panting but pleased.

"We need to travel incognito from now on," he told Evie, gesturing to the bag. "People bring their pets on the train sometimes, but they have to be in bags."

Evie wrinkled her nose. "Really? Did Bitsy carry you in a bag?"

Bart almost laughed. "Are you kidding? Bitsy DuPont has never used the subway. But trust me, I've been down here a lot. I know what I'm talking about." He lifted his head, gesturing to the sign hanging over them. "These trains all go up to Harlem. All we have to do is wait for the next one to come!"

"Wow! You're brilliant!" Evie exclaimed. Or at least, that's what Bart told himself she said. A train was screeching to a halt not far down the platform, and it was hard to hear the bunny over the racket.

Bart watched the train slow as it rolled closer to

him and Evie. "Hop in the bag," he told her. "I'll get us inside. Then we'll both just hang out in the bag until we get to your stop."

Evie obeyed immediately, and as the train doors opened, Bart dragged the bag inside. The seats were mostly full, with a few people standing, and everyone was too engrossed in phones or books or conversations to pay any attention to the dog with the tote bag. Bart spotted a gray-haired man in a business suit dozing in the seat near the door. *Bingo*, he thought, nudging the bag closer to his feet before climbing in to join Evie. If anyone noticed them, they would just assume the man had brought his dog and bunny to work in a tote bag. Nothing weird about that, right? Well, not in New York City, anyway.

The doors slid closed, the train lurched forward, and soon they were speeding through the tunnel. After the next stop, Bart started to relax. It was working! Only two stops to go.

At the second stop, a group of teenagers piled

on, talking excitedly. Bart and Evie stayed perfectly still.

At the third stop, the businessman came awake with a snort and got off the train. Cringing, Bart tried to scoot the tote bag farther back under the seats. One of the teenagers, a girl with loads of curly hair, glanced down—then did a double take.

No! Bart thought frantically, but it was too late.

"Aw, there's a puppy in that bag!" the girl exclaimed. "Where's your owner, little guy?"

"Hang on, there's something else in there," a boy with a baseball cap said. Bart flinched as he nudged the bag gently with his sneaker, revealing a cowering Evie.

The girl gasped. "A bunny!" Delighted, she snapped a photo of them with her phone.

Another girl, this one with a shaved head, grabbed the boy's arm. "Hang on," she said loudly. Bart glanced nervously around the car and realized the girl had everyone's attention. "Is that the dog and bunny from Twitter?"

"What?" a woman sitting near the door said, half standing out of her seat.

"It is!" The girl was practically yelling now. "It's Bunny and Canine!"

"You're right!" the boy said, his eyes huge. "That's totally them!"

Oh no, Bart thought as everyone scrambled to pull out their phones. The train began to slow, and Bart tensed.

"Run!" he shouted. He and Evie burst out of the bag, dodging around legs as the doors slid open, and then they sprinted onto a new platform and headed for the stairs.

16

 EVIE

Evie saw daylight at the top of the steps and put on a burst of speed. The subway station might have been dark and underground, but it was *not* ideal for burrowing. As she and Bart raced back up onto the street in the bright sunlight, Evie felt a wave of relief.

And then another, even more powerful wave of familiarity.

"Harlem!" she cried, turning in a quick circle. This wasn't the street JAL Corner Deli was on, but still—it looked and smelled like home. They were so close!

"We made it!" Bart agreed. And then, to Evie's surprise, he stuck his nose between her ears and took a big whiff.

"What are you doing?" Evie yelped, hopping away.

"Getting your scent," Bart explained. "Your bodega will have your scent, so now all we have to do is let my nose lead us there!"

Evie was impressed. "Then let's go!"

They set off, Bart sniffing the ground intently, Evie doing her best to follow while staying out of sight. This street wasn't too busy, with just a few pedestrians here and there, and soon they reached an intersection. Bart paused, *sniff sniff sniff*, and then veered right.

They passed block after block, and Evie was starting to pant. Bart was moving faster and faster, and it was getting hard to keep up.

Suddenly, something small and plump and red on the sidewalk caught Evie's eye. Was that . . . it was! A raspberry!

Evie's belly rumbled. Keeping an eye on Bart, she darted over and gobbled down the raspberry. It was tart and sweet and absolutely *delicious*. Evie hurried forward—she'd have to really run to catch up with Bart now—but then she spotted another raspberry!

Evie knew she couldn't fall behind, especially now that Bart was moving so fast. But she couldn't resist pausing to chow down on that raspberry, too. And a few feet away, another one. And another, and another!

"Bart!" Evie tried to call out, her cheeks bulging with yummy berries. One last raspberry lay on the ground near an alley. Promising herself she'd catch up to Bart after this, Evie pounced on the berry. A shadow moved in the alley, and before Evie could even swallow, a pair of hands reached down and snatched her up.

17

 LAURA

Laura and her cousins sat huddled around a table, each girl staring intently at her phone while music blasted from the DJ's speakers. They were seated as far away as possible from the dance floor, where Laura's parents and Uncle Hector and Aunt Ana were apparently competing to see who had the most embarrassing moves.

"Status update," Bianca said suddenly. She'd taken charge of Mission Bodega Bunny, giving each girl an assignment.

"No new videos," Grace replied, swiping her

screen. Her job was monitoring #BunnyandCanine on Twitter for the most recent sightings.

"No responses yet," Izzy said. She had followed New York City Animal Services on Twitter, Facebook, and Instagram, and was leaving messages and replies on all three asking if anyone had brought in a Shiba Inu or a gray bunny.

"Laura, how about you?" Bianca asked.

Laura sighed. "No responses for me, either."

She stared glumly at the two tweets she'd sent out almost an hour ago.

@JALBodegaBunny: FYI, put out some raspberries and I might come say hi! (If I do, please let my very worried owner know by responding to this tweet)

"Someone will respond," Izzy said with complete confidence. "I just know it, Laura."

Laura tried to smile. Her cousins were being so nice and so helpful. She couldn't help but feel guilty when she thought about how much she'd dreaded spending this weekend with them.

"I bet you're right," she said.

Bianca studied Laura thoughtfully. "You know, I bet a lot more people would get involved if you made a video."

Grace gasped. "Ooh, *yes*! That's a great idea!"

Laura's stomach twisted. "What kind of video?"

"Just, like . . ." Bianca waved her hand vaguely. "You talking about Evie, how worried you are, and asking people to help."

"But I already did that!" Laura said.

"Yeah, but that's just one tweet in a hashtag with like a billion other tweets," Izzy chimed in. "If people actually saw your face, if they saw *you* and heard you talk about how much you love Evie, they'd definitely want to help!"

For a moment, Laura felt a twinge of annoyance. This was the dance routine at their family reunion all over again! She didn't *want* to be on video, especially not when thousands of people might see!

Then Laura thought of Evie, frightened and lost in the city. As much as she hated to admit it, her cousins were probably right—a video had a much better chance of going viral. And even though the idea of being in a viral video made her feel queasy and slightly light-headed, shouldn't Laura do everything she possibly could to find Evie?

She looked at her cousins' eager faces and took a deep breath.

"Okay. I'm in."

"Yes!" Grace cheered.

"Let's film it now!" Izzy exclaimed, jumping up.

Laura stiffened immediately, and she willed her pulse to slow. But before she had a chance to think about what she was going to say, Bianca half stood out of her chair, her eyes on her phone.

"Hang on, Izzy—there's a new photo!"

"What is it?" Laura cried, leaning over to see. Bianca extended her arms, holding her phone out so that all four girls could see the screen. Laura's heart fluttered with excitement. The photo was taken in a subway car, where a tote bag lay underneath a seat. And just visible inside the bag were two familiar furry faces.

"That's them!" she exclaimed, and her cousins cheered. "Did someone tweet that? What else did they say?"

Tapping the screen, Grace cleared her throat and read out loud. "Spotted #BunnyandCanine on the 2 train! They ran off at 125th. No sign of the necklace."

"No necklace?" Izzy sounded disappointed. "Aw, I guess they lost it."

"Or ate it," Grace said, giggling. "Remember when Marissa's puppy swallowed her whole entire collar?"

Laura was barely listening. She gazed at Grace's screen, reading the tweet over and over again. After a minute, Bianca nudged her.

"What is it?" she asked.

Finally, Laura smiled for real. "They got off at 125th Street," she told her cousins. "This might sound ridiculous, but . . . I think Evie's trying to go home."

18

 BART

Bart tore up the street, tail high in the air. Like any neighborhood in Manhattan, Harlem had thousands of smells—currently, Bart was catching strong whiffs of raw fish, pineapple, bus exhaust, and fabric softener—but none of those mattered. Bart was in the zone now. Evie's scent was like a single thread in the complicated fabric of the city, but Bart's nose had caught it and he wasn't about to let it go. One more block up, then a sharp right, and—

"There!" Bart came to an abrupt halt, wagging furiously. Just across the street was a convenience store with a green-and-yellow awning . . . but it was clearly locked up tight.

Wuh-oh. Bart turned, expecting to see Evie looking totally devastated. But she wasn't there.

"Evie?" Bart looked up and down the street, fur rising on his back. He'd been so focused on finding Evie's home, he hadn't realized the bunny wasn't behind him anymore!

Bart raced around the corner and darted around a woman pushing a stroller. There! For a moment, Bart felt a wave of relief at the sight of Evie crouched down at the end of the block, nibbling something red. *So she stopped for a snack*, he thought with amusement. Maybe there was hope for her after all.

Then, quick as lightning, a pair of arms reached down from the alley and snatched Evie up!

With a frantic yelp, Bart raced down the street. He veered into the alley, but it appeared empty. Bart spun in a circle, barking at the top of his lungs. "Evie? Evie, where are you? Ev—*ack!*"

A steel loop slipped around Bart's head and

pulled. Bart yanked and tugged, but he couldn't get free. Finally, he turned around and found himself staring up at Jeff the dogcatcher, holding the pole attached to the steel loop in one hand. And in his other hand . . .

"Evie," Bart groaned, but it came out a whimper.

"Got you at last, little guy!" Jeff looked extremely pleased. "All I needed was the right bait. Well, that and a lot of helpful tips on Twitter. You two are pretty famous!"

Evie wouldn't meet Bart's gaze. Her long ears were completely flat, her whiskers drooping. Bart had no choice but to follow Jeff out of the alley and toward the dogcatcher truck. He couldn't believe they'd gotten caught this close to Evie's home. Although, maybe it was best that she didn't see it all locked up that way. Her family really was gone. Still, she deserved better than the shelter, especially since it was Bart's fault she'd been caught.

But he could make things right.

Bart jumped obediently into the crate in the

back of the truck. He turned around as Jeff reached out to put Evie beside him—and nipped Jeff on the arm.

"Hey!" Jeff yelped, dropping Evie. She landed nimbly on the ground and stared up at Bart with wide eyes.

"Run!" Bart shouted just as Jeff slammed his crate door closed. Evie blinked, and Jeff started to reach for her. "Evie, *now!*"

This time, she listened. As the gray bunny tore off down the street, Bart let out a sigh of relief. Evie was a wild bunny now, whether she liked it or not.

But for Bart, the wild life was over.

19

 EVIE

Evie darted beneath a hot dog vendor's cart and peered out from behind a wheel. She watched the dogcatcher's legs slow to a halt only a few feet away, then turn in a circle. Holding her breath, Evie remained perfectly still until, at last, the dogcatcher headed back to his truck.

She poked her head out from under the cart. The dogcatcher pulled out a set of keys, then closed the back of the truck. But not before Evie caught a final glimpse of Bart behind bars.

He'd saved her. And now he was locked up.

The dogcatcher climbed into the driver's seat of the truck, and a moment later, the engine roared to life. Evie's pulse raced, and she was shaking all over. But after a moment, she realized it wasn't fear she felt anymore. She was *mad.*

She wouldn't let this happen to Bart.

Without giving herself a chance to think about how completely and totally dangerous it might be, Evie tore out from under the cart. As the truck pulled away from the curb and into the street, Evie raced alongside it on the sidewalk. The light at the next intersection was green, but traffic was still moving slowly. Evie moved to the curb so that she'd have a clear view of the truck. She darted around a massive pile of garbage bags and saw the truck's brake lights glow red. The car behind it slowed, too, and Evie knew this would be the best chance she'd get.

She launched herself between the car and the truck. Already, the brake lights had stopped glowing, and the truck was picking up speed. Not daring to look back at the car behind her, Evie ran full speed—then leaped as far as she could.

"*Oof!*" She landed on the bumper and pressed her whole body against the closed door. There was nothing to hold on to, but the little ledge offered just enough space for her to huddle. The truck was moving even faster now, and the wind rippled Evie's fur. She watched as block after block whizzed by, brick buildings and restaurant patios, buses and motorcycles and taxis, people walking, buying ice cream cones, selling paintings and records and sunglasses from little booths on the street . . .

Evie remembered how scared she'd been just yesterday, hunkered down in her crate inside a subway car. At the time, it had been the most traumatizing thing that had ever happened to her. Now here she was, clinging to the back of a truck heading toward the animal shelter. And she wasn't traumatized at all.

If anything, she felt free.

* * *

The moment the truck parked and the engine shut off, Evie hopped off and hurried to hide behind a large cinder block. She watched as the dogcatcher climbed out of the truck, opened the back, and pulled Bart's crate out.

"Hang on, Bart," Evie whispered as the dog-catcher carried the crate over to a bright blue door. "I'm coming."

The dogcatcher swiped a card in front of a panel, and the door opened. He stepped inside, and Evie sprang forward as the door began to close, but . . .

"No!" Evie cried as the door clicked shut. Desperate, she looked around, hoping someone else with one of those cards might approach. But the truck was parked in a small lot behind the shelter, and there was no one in sight.

Evie hurried around to the front of the building. A woman wearing the same uniform as the dogcatcher was visible inside the glass double doors, locking up.

Groaning, Evie retreated back to the parking lot. Now she couldn't get inside until tomorrow morning. And that meant she was on her own tonight. At least she didn't have to worry about dinner, not with all the raspberries in her belly. Evie spotted a dumpster and squeezed behind it. It was smelly and not the most comfortable hiding spot, but it would do until morning.

All Evie could think about was how sad Bart had looked when the dogcatcher had slammed the crate closed. He must be so lonely and frightened right now . . . just like Evie had been when he'd found her.

It was hours before Evie finally drifted off into a troubled sleep.

The sound of a car door slamming jolted Evie awake the next morning.

Cautiously, she peered around the dumpster. The same woman she'd seen close the shelter last night was walking away from her car. As Evie watched, she swiped a card over the panel and the door swung open.

Evie almost darted out, but then another car pulled into the parking lot. Then another, and another. The shelter workers greeted one another, sipping from paper cups with black lids as they filed inside. The door locked shut behind them, and Evie finally emerged from her spot.

She hurried to the front of the building and hung back as a man holding a little girl's hand walked toward the front entrance. The glass double doors slid open as they approached, and Evie didn't hesitate—she scurried in after them.

She quickly found refuge behind a trash can and took a look at her surroundings. There was a big desk with several people standing behind it, all of them wearing the same shirt the dogcatcher had been wearing. A few people waited in front of the desk, some of them filling out paperwork. As Evie watched, a woman with twin boys handed her papers back to the guy behind the desk. He gave her a big smile and said, "Congratulations! I'm so glad Chipper has found such a great home."

That's when Evie saw the tiny black pit bull puppy one of the little boys was holding. His curly tail wagged fiercely as the boy hugged him closer.

Evie looked at the line of people again and realized almost all of them had a dog or a cat, some in crates, others in their arms or on leashes. They were all getting adopted, going to new homes.

For a moment, Evie doubted her own plan. Was that why Bart was here? To find a new family? Surely that would be the best thing for him, wouldn't it?

But Bart loved his life of freedom on the streets. He'd risked everything to try to help Evie go home. She owed him . . . and his home was roaming free in Manhattan.

Cautiously, Evie crept out from behind the trash can. She stuck to the wall, making her way toward another set of double doors. Behind them was a cacophony of barks, whines, whimpers, and yowls. Steeling herself, Evie waited until no one was looking, then ran up to the doors and pushed with all her might. To her surprise, the doors gave easily, swinging just enough to let her in.

"Whoa." Evie gaped at the sight in front of her. Row after row after row of crates, each one holding a dog or cat. Unlike Evie's cozy hutch, these crates were mostly empty save for a water bowl and a toy. Some of the animals were curled into a ball, fast asleep. Others sat up, alert and curious as the occasional person walked by. Several cats loudly mewled their discontent, while a few of the bigger dogs, wiggling with excitement, stood on their hind legs and pawed at the crate doors, barking at anyone who passed.

Evie swallowed. How was she ever going to find Bart? There must be hundreds of dogs here!

Just then, someone appeared at the end of the main aisle. Evie tensed as she recognized the dog-catcher who had captured Bart—only he didn't have Bart anymore, just that stick with the loop at the end.

Evie perked up. Maybe he'd put Bart in one of the crates in that last row! She waited until the dogcatcher had disappeared through a door, then scurried as fast as she could down the aisle. Almost every dog she passed went wild at the sight of her, but Evie didn't flinch. She turned down the last row and slowed just enough to get a good look at every dog. It was only a matter of time before the dogcatcher or another worker came to see what all the ruckus was about.

"Bart?" she called, but her tiny voice was lost under all the barking. Then, in the last crate at the end of the row: *"Bart!"*

She almost didn't recognize her friend. The Shiba Inu was curled into a ball, making him look much smaller than he was. His black nose rested on his paws, and his eyes were closed. He looked completely and utterly defeated.

"Bart!" Evie yelled again, batting the door with her paw. She heard voices over the barking now, and they were getting closer.

Bart opened one eye. Then he sprang up in surprise. *"Evie?!"*

"Hang on!" Evie said, studying the latch on the door. It was a lot like the latch on her hutch. She bit down on the top of the latch, which moved down just a little bit. Then she pushed the button with her paw, and . . .

"Yes!" she cried. The door sprang open, and Bart stared in amazement.

"How did you—"

"No time for that!" Evie said urgently. "Come on!"

Together, the two of them raced out of the row and down another wide aisle, ducking into another row when a pair of footsteps sounded ahead. Evie's heart thrummed with excitement as she and Bart zigzagged their way back to the double doors. All they had to do now was get across that lobby, and they were home free!

Evie stopped outside the doors and peered through. "I don't think there's any way for us to get across without being seen. We should just run for the doors as fast as we can."

"Evie?"

Something about Bart's tone caught her attention. Evie looked back at Bart, who was eyeing her almost nervously. "What's wrong?"

"I really appreciate you breaking me out like this," Bart said. "And I know you want me to help you get home. But . . . well, I found it. Your bodega. And it's all locked up. Your family is gone."

Evie blinked several times. Disappointment coursed through her but also surprise. "Wait. Bart, do you think I came to get you just so you'd take me home?"

"Well, yeah."

"But that's not why I did it," Evie told him. The truth was, when Bart had been loaded up onto the truck, she hadn't even thought about home. "I did it because you're my friend, and I was trying to help you find *your* home. Or, I guess . . . our home."

Bart stared at her. His ears perked up. "Wait, really? You want to live on the streets, too?"

Evie thought about Laura and felt an intense

pang of sadness. But Laura was gone, and Evie had done everything she could to get home. Maybe it was time to move on.

"I do," she said. "Ready?"

Bart's tail wagged frantically. "Ready!"

"*Go!*"

The two of them burst through the double doors and raced across the lobby. A few children gasped and pointed, and heads started to turn in their direction. But Evie stayed focused on those doors. They were so close now, so close to freedom, just a few more feet and then—

"*Heel!*"

The sharp voice sliced through the air. Next to Evie, Bart skidded to a halt so fast he lost his balance and bumped into her. Evie stumbled, rolling over and staring as Bart sat up straight, nose high in the air, every muscle tense.

"What are you doing?" Evie hissed. And then she saw the tall, beady-eyed woman with gray hair pulled back in a tight bun from the park—the one who'd lost her diamond collar while she was busy snapping at her fluffy white dog.

Now her fierce gaze was focused on Bart. And suddenly, Evie realized why Bart had been so panicked when he'd seen the diamonds. He wasn't upset that Evie had found a collar for him. He was upset because he knew to whom it belonged.

Bitsy DuPont.

20

 LAURA

"I wish you could stay longer!" Grace wailed when Laura stepped off the elevator with her suitcase. "Mom, Dad, can Laura come visit again? Oooh, maybe for Thanksgiving?"

"Mom makes the best pernil," Izzy told Laura. "And last year I made pumpkin flan!"

"It was actually pretty good," Bianca admitted.

Aunt Ana raised an eyebrow at Dad. "Not a bad idea, eh, Jorge?"

Dad looked at Laura, and she knew he expected her to wrinkle her nose or give a little shake of her

189

head. Some polite way of saying no without actually *saying* it. The Rodriguez family had always celebrated Thanksgiving at home together, just the three of them—four, with Evie. It was quiet and relaxing, and Laura loved it.

But to her surprise as much as Dad's, Laura heard herself say, "That would be awesome!"

Dad's eyes widened. He turned to Aunt Ana with a big smile. "A big family Thanksgiving sounds like a great idea!"

Laura's cousins cheered and surrounded her in a bone-crushing group hug.

"Tell us the second Evie's home, okay?" Grace begged.

"We'll keep Mission Bodega Bunny going until you find her!" Bianca added.

Izzy's eyes lit up. "Maybe you can bring her to Thanksgiving!"

Tears pricked Laura's eyes as she hugged them back. "That's a great idea. I can't wait to see you all again."

And she meant it.

* * *

The flight home seemed to last forever. Laura used the in-flight Wi-Fi to check Twitter obsessively.

Her video about Evie had almost ten thousand retweets.

Every time Laura thought about it, she felt a strange swoop in her stomach, like a roller coaster drop. The video was only half a minute long, and Laura's voice shook a little bit as she described Evie and asked for help finding her. But Bianca had been right—suddenly, *everyone* wanted to help.

Reading through their responses made Laura feel better. They were all so encouraging, promising to spread the word, some even pledging to carry raspberries around with them until Evie was found. It warmed Laura's heart to see that so many strangers in the city were coming together to help find her lost pet.

Laura's parents loved the video, too. And while Laura had told them about Evie riding the subway, she hadn't told them she thought Evie was trying to go home. She knew what their reaction would be: sympathetic smiles, "maybes" that really meant "probably not." Mom and Dad wouldn't want Laura to get her hopes up.

But as their cab pulled up to JAL Corner Deli, Laura's heart was racing with excitement. She was so sure—she was *absolutely positive*—that Evie would be waiting for her. The Shiba Inu, too, fluffy tail wagging with pride, ready for Laura to shower him with praise and treats.

Laura looked up and down the street as Dad unlocked the grate and rolled it up. She resisted the urge to call Evie's name. The bells jangled as Dad pushed the door open, and Laura stepped inside.

The store was dark and quiet, just as they'd left it. Laura hurried down aisle three and checked behind the sugar bags. No Evie. She could feel Mom and Dad watching her, but she didn't care anymore.

Leaving her suitcase in the store, Laura raced up the stairs to their apartment. "Evie? Evie!" she called, checking all Evie's hiding places—the pantry, the cupboards, behind the toilet. Finally, she burst into her room and peered first under the bed, then in her closet. No Evie. Laura sank down on the edge of her bed and stared at the space on the floor where Evie's hutch was supposed to be. Her eyes filled with tears, and she squeezed them closed. Maybe she shouldn't have gotten her hopes up after all.

Footsteps sounded in the hall, and Laura cringed. She didn't want to talk to anyone right now. A moment later, she heard a familiar ringtone—her mom's phone. The footsteps stopped.

"Hello?" Mom said. She was right outside Laura's door. "Oh, hi, Blair!"

Laura sat up straight, her pulse quickening. She hurried to the door and threw it open. Mom met her eyes but held up a finger that said *hang on*.

"Yes, we just got home. We . . . What's that?" Mom blinked. Then a slow smile spread across her face, and Laura felt hope rise up in her chest once again. "Yes—yes, of course! We'll be right there!"

21

 BART

Every muscle in Bart's body was rigid. Even his heart seemed to have stopped beating. He stared up into his former owner's face, her expression pinched into her usual frown, and felt all his hope drain away. It was like his life as a wild, free dog had never happened. When Bitsy DuPont gave a command, Bart obeyed. He couldn't help it. He'd been trained too well.

He could hear Evie whispering urgently behind him, but he couldn't make out what she was saying. He wanted to tell her to run, get away, save herself.

But his owner had said *heel*, and now Bart had to stick by her side. Even if he could turn and try to explain that to Evie, she'd never understand. Her Laura probably never drilled her for hours at a time, running commands over and over again. She probably didn't even know a single command.

Everyone in the lobby had gone still and quiet. They watched as Bitsy walked up to the counter as if there was no line at all. Bart trotted obediently at her side, sitting when she came to a stop. He hoped Evie had fled, but he suspected she was still there, staring at him.

"Um, can I help you?" the woman behind the counter said, glancing curiously from Bitsy to Bart.

Bitsy sniffed haughtily. "I am Bitsy DuPont, of DuPont's Champion Dogs," she announced loudly enough for the entire lobby to hear. "And this," she went on, gesturing vaguely at Bart, "is my former show dog, Bartholomew Porpington the Third. He ran away last year, and one of your dogcatchers notified me that he'd been picked up."

Murmurs and whispers rippled through the crowd. *Evie, please, please get out of here before it's too late,* Bart thought fervently.

"I see," the woman said, but she sounded confused. "So . . . so you're here to claim your lost dog? That's wonderful, I'm so—"

"Hardly," Bitsy interrupted. Bart blinked, but he kept his gaze fixed straight ahead. "DuPont dogs are obedient. They are champions. They do as they're told. And they certainly do not run away. I tried to do this over the phone, but your dogcatcher told me it must be done in person, and so I am here to surrender this dog to the shelter—officially. He is no dog of mine."

Bart couldn't believe his ears. He tried to keep still, but his tail twitched just a little bit.

"Oh." The woman's expression changed, and now she regarded Bitsy with a sour look. "All right, then. In that case, I have some papers for you to sign."

The hushed voices behind Bart sounded

sympathetic, and he imagined everyone staring at him with pity. The poor dog whose owner no longer wanted him. But Bart had never felt so happy in his life. As Bitsy signed the last paper, he half expected her to change her mind, leash him up, take him home, and force him back into his old life.

But she simply put the pen down and sauntered out of the shelter without so much as a glance back in his direction.

Bart felt like he'd just come out of a trance. He whirled around and was unsurprised to see Evie still there, staring at him with wide eyes. His tail *thwap-thwap-thwapped* against the floor. They were free! Except . . .

Gulping, Bart looked up. All eyes in the lobby were on him. Including two more shelter workers who had just come through the doors that led to the back.

"I can't believe it," came a voice near the front door. To Bart's surprise, the dogcatcher stood there, regarding him sadly. "I thought she'd be so thrilled to have him back. Especially now that he's a Twitter star!"

"He is?" another shelter worker asked.

The dogcatcher grinned. "Yeah! That's Bunny and Canine!"

A few laughs broke out, and Bart saw several people reach for their phones.

"Well, it's not often we get celebrities here!" the woman behind the counter said cheerfully. "Don't worry, you two. I'm sure we'll find you both great homes in no time."

Homes. Bart saw from Evie's horrified expression that she was thinking the same thing he was. They would be separated, sent to live with different families. Panic rippled through Bart. Somehow, the thought of never seeing Evie again was even worse than the idea of losing his wild street life. He bounded toward Evie just as the shelter workers stepped forward. One of them lifted Evie, and she twisted and thrashed in his arms.

Bart jumped up, placing his paws on the worker's waist, gazing up at him with his most pleading puppy-dog eyes. And then a new voice cried out from the entrance:

"That's my bunny!"

22

 EVIE

Evie couldn't believe her ears. Squirming in the shelter worker's grip, she managed to turn toward the entrance. Mr. and Mrs. Rodriguez were there, and so was Mrs. Vanderwaal. And in front of them, hands on her hips and eyes blazing, was *Laura*.

Her fierceness caught Evie off guard. Every single person in the whole lobby was looking right at Laura, something that would normally make her blush and flee the room, maybe even in tears. But something had obviously changed, because this Laura didn't even seem to notice the crowd's attention. She almost looked ready to fight for Evie.

Realization dawned, and warmth spread from Evie's ears all the way to her paws. Laura had never meant to abandon her or give her to a new owner. She was still, and would always be, Evie's family.

With a final wiggle, Evie broke free of the worker's hold and bounded across the lobby, leaping into Laura's arms.

"Evie!" Laura cried, cuddling her close. "I missed you so, *so* much!"

I missed you, too, Evie thought. But as happy as she felt, something still wasn't right. Evie's heart twinged when she looked down and saw Bart gazing up at her. His expression was hard to read, his eyes filled with sadness and something like wonder. After a moment, Evie realized why.

All this time, Evie couldn't understand why Bart didn't want a home and a family. But now that she'd met Bitsy DuPont, she completely understood. The woman was cruel and cold and she might have taken care of Bart, but she certainly never loved him. And

201

that was the only owner Bart had ever known. No wonder he thought Evie would like life on the streets better than life with Laura! But now that Bart actually saw Laura and how much she loved Evie, he was starting to understand what he'd been missing out on all along.

Suddenly, Evie knew exactly what she had to do.

"Evie!" Laura exclaimed as the bunny wiggled from her grasp. Evie scurried over to Bart and sat next to him, staring up at Laura unblinkingly.

"What are you doing?" Bart whispered, but Evie didn't respond. She just willed Laura to understand what she was trying to communicate.

Laura's brow furrowed for a second. Then her expression cleared, and hope surged through Evie. Spinning around, Laura faced her parents.

"Mom, Dad—this dog saved Evie's life! And now he needs a home, too."

Mr. and Mrs. Rodriguez looked at each other. After a moment, they both smiled and turned back to their daughter.

"I suppose it couldn't hurt for the bodega to have *two* mascots," Mr. Rodriguez said.

"Really?" Laura squealed, throwing her arms around him. "Thank you, thank you, *thank* you!" She faced Evie and Bart again, smiling from ear to ear. "Hey, boy. How'd you like to come home with us?"

Bart sat perfectly still. His gaze flicked over to Evie's, and she held her breath. Then he let out a short, happy "Ruff!" and licked Laura's hand.

Laura's parents and Mrs. Vanderwaal laughed, and the dogcatcher wiped away a tear. As Evie watched Laura scratch Bart behind the ears, she felt overcome with a joy so powerful, she couldn't sit still one second longer. Evie leaped straight up, twirling in midair.

"She's doing a binky!" Laura cried, pulling out her phone and taking a video as Evie leaped and twirled again and again. She saw Bart gazing at her, looking impressed—and then he joined in!

Everyone watching burst out laughing at the sight

of the bunny and the dog spinning in the air like ballerinas.

"Those two really do belong together," Laura's dad said, grinning.

Evie couldn't have agreed more.

23

 LAURA

Four months later . . .

"Dad, where are those new snickerdoodle cookies?" Laura called, hands on her hips as she surveyed
aisle seven. "I want to bring a package to book
club!"

"Display case at the front!" Dad called back. He
was behind the register, ringing up Mr. Patel's usual
peach tea, spearmint gum, and newspaper.

"Thanks!" Laura squeezed past a man selecting a
bag of pretzels and hurried to the front of the store.

A group of teenagers stood around the display, and for a moment, Laura wondered why they were cooing over cookies. Then she saw Evie.

Her bunny was nestled in a little basket right in the middle of the display table, which gave her a view of the busy street outside the window. It was just one of the many changes Laura had noticed ever since Evie's Manhattan adventure—she hardly ever hid behind the sugar bags anymore.

"Hey!" a girl with a shaved head said to Laura. "These guys are yours, right?"

She pointed, and Laura felt the familiar flutter of anxiety at the sudden attention—although it was much fainter now than it used to be. Taking a deep breath, Laura peered around the table and laughed. Bart was flat on his back in front of the table, tail wagging fiercely as another girl scratched his belly.

"Yup, they are."

"Awesome!" The first girl grinned at Laura. "I follow these guys on Twitter. Your pics are great."

"Thanks!" Laura said. After adopting Bart, she'd changed @JALBodegaBunny to @BunnyandCanine. The account had over twenty thousand followers and counting!

"We actually met them before, sort of," one of the boys told Laura. "We were on the 2 train when they were hiding in that tote bag! You know, right after they stole that diamond necklace."

"Oh, wow!" Laura exclaimed. "You tweeted a photo of them, right? I saw that!"

"Whatever happened with that necklace?" said the girl crouched down on the floor with Bart. "Did they ever find it?"

"I don't think so," Laura said, shrugging. She picked up a package of snickerdoodle cookies and slid it into her backpack, right next to her copy of *The River's End*. She couldn't wait to tell everyone at book club her theory about the witch queen's sister and what might happen in the sequel.

"My brother's coming home for Thanksgiving next week," the girl with the shaved head told Laura.

"He said the first thing he wants to do is meet Bunny and Canine."

Laura laughed. "Cool! Although we're going to be closed for a few days. We're going to Florida, so these two are staying with a friend downtown."

Mrs. Vanderwaal was excited about having the famous duo as guests—and she'd promised fervently to make sure the door would stay closed. But Laura wasn't worried. She knew Evie and Bart would be just fine.

Laura picked Evie up and gave her a quick snuggle. Then she knelt down to rub Bart behind the ears. His new collar was bright red—nothing fancy, but he seemed to like it.

"See you guys in a few hours!" she said, shouldering her backpack. Waving to the teens still crowded around Evie and Bart, Laura stepped out of the bodega and headed off to book club.

EPILOGUE

"Oh, Wentworth!" Mrs. Vanderwaal called in a sing-song voice. She struggled to hold the cardboard box in her arms steady as she entered her apartment, kicking the door closed behind her. "You'll never guess what I've got!"

Teeny, high-pitched mews sounded from the box as Mrs. Vanderwaal set it carefully on the floor. "Wentworth? Wentworth!" She sighed, shaking her head at the three fluffy gray-and-white kittens inside the box. "I think your new foster brother is out scavenging again," she said, reaching inside to stroke their soft ears. "Why don't you three wait right here, and I'll get your lunch ready?"

Smiling, she stood up and headed into the kitchen.

Inside the box, one kitten busied himself licking his paw. The second curled up into a tight ball and fell fast asleep. But the third felt wide awake and excited. What was outside this box? She couldn't wait to find out!

Her brother let out an irritated "mrowr" as she scrambled up on his back, stretching as high as she could. Her claws gripped the edge of the box, and her back legs scrabbled up the side. She was up, up, up—and over the side!

The kitten tumbled to the floor, extremely pleased with herself. She could hear Mrs. Vanderwaal whistling in the room to the right, so she decided to head off in the other direction to explore. Every inch of the place was spotless, everything smelled clean and new, except . . .

Pausing, the kitten sniffed. Was that tuna? She followed the scent, squeezing through a crack in a slightly open door and finding herself in a small room. Her eyes went wide and round with wonder.

The pavilion was beautiful, all curvy dark wood and red velvet, topped with a golden egg covered in green and purple jewels. Behind the parted curtains, the kitten could see a plush bed inside. She climbed in and gazed around in amazement. The place was a treasure trove: chicken bones, a fancy shoe, and all sorts of things the kitten had never seen before. She caught sight of an open tuna can and hurried over eagerly. It was mostly empty, but she happily lapped up the tuna water at the bottom. As she did, a glimmer caught her eye.

Abandoning the can, the kitten climbed over the fancy shoe and pushed aside a banana peel. There, tucked away at the very back of the pavilion, was the most beautiful thing the kitten had ever laid eyes on.

I am going to love *living here*, she thought, gently taking the diamond collar with her teeth. Then she hurried out of the pavilion to search for the perfect hiding place.

AUTHOR'S NOTE

Social anxiety is a normal part of growing up. If you struggle with anxiety just like Laura and Evie, you aren't alone! Talk to your parents or guardians about how you feel. There are lots of resources out there for your family that can help you manage your anxiety and overcome your fears. Here are a few to start with:

Anxiety and Depression Association of America: https://adaa.org/living-with-anxiety/children

Association for Behavioral and Cognitive Therapies: http://www.abct.org/Information/?m=mInformation&fa=fs_ANXIETY

Child Mind Institute: https://childmind.org/topics/concerns/anxiety/

ACKNOWLEDGMENTS

A giant thank-you to my editor, Orlando Dos Reis, and to my agent, Sarah Davies, for always sharing their wisdom, insights, and cute animal pics. I'd also like to thank everyone at Scholastic, including Amanda Maciel, Keirsten Geise, Caroline Flanagan, and Jackie Hornberger.

Special thanks to Dr. Rachel Busman at the Child Mind Institute for reading this book and providing such helpful and thoughtful notes on childhood anxiety. Finally, thank you to all of the workers and volunteers at animal shelters and rescue organizations who help so many Barts and Evies find their families!

ABOUT THE AUTHOR

Michelle Schusterman is the author of over a dozen books for kids and teens, including *Spell & Spindle, Olive and the Backstage Ghost*, and the series The Kat Sinclair Files and I Heart Band. She's also the co-author of the Secrets of Topsea series under the name M. Shelley Coats. She currently resides in Dallas with her husband and their polar bear masquerading as a Lab puppy.